WHOM SHALL I SERVE?

KEIRA'S DARK SOUL

MG. WILLIAMS

iUniverse®

WHOM SHALL I SERVE?
KEIRA'S DARK SOUL

iUniverse books may be ordered through booksellers or by contacting:

iUniverse
1663 Liberty Drive
Bloomington, IN 47403
www.iuniverse.com
844-349-9409

Because of the dynamic nature of the Internet, any web addresses or links contained in this book may have changed since publication and may no longer be valid. The views expressed in this work are solely those of the author and do not necessarily reflect the views of the publisher, and the publisher hereby disclaims any responsibility for them.

Any people depicted in stock imagery provided by Getty Images are models, and such images are being used for illustrative purposes only. Certain stock imagery © Getty Images.

ISBN: 978-1-6632-4059-0 (sc)
ISBN: 978-1-6632-4058-3 (e)

Library of Congress Control Number: 2022911051

Print information available on the last page.

iUniverse rev. date: 06/30/2022

CONTENTS

Chapter 1 Chaos 1

Chapter 2 Death and Deception 4

Chapter 3 The Lies Begin 6

Chapter 4 Wedding Day Blues.................................. 14

Chapter 5 The Blue Lady Has Come 23

Chapter 6 The Guardian 27

Chapter 7 Looking for Dirt 33

Chapter 8 To Close for Comfort 37

Chapter 9 Celestial Birth...46

Chapter 10 Uninvited Guest...52

Chapter 11 New Dawn 61

Chapter 12 New Wisdom and Power 68

Chapter 13 Do Not Be Deceived.................................73

Chapter 14 Broken Curse 81

Chapter 15 Lesson Learned..89

Chapter 16 Reckless 93

Chapter 17 Unexpected Outcomes 98

Chapter 18 Cooking with a Bang.............................. 106

Chapter 19 Best Friend or Lover?............................. 110

Chapter 20 Masquerade Ball...................................... 114

Chapter 21 Fight or Flight.. 125

Chapter 22 The Battle Begins.................................... 129

Chapter 23 Three's company...................................... 133

Chapter 24 Something is Coming.............................. 137

Chapter 25 Strategy of War 141

Chapter 26 Mirror, Mirror Take me Home.................. 147

Chapter 27 Perilous Gathering 154

Chapter 28 Somber Graduation 159

Chapter 29 Diary Secrets 163

Chapter 30 The Unexpected 175
Chapter 31 Closer Than Anticipated........................... 186
Chapter 32 Romantic Interlude Gone Wrong 191
Chapter 33 The Enemy Has Returned 197
Chapter 34 Last-Minute Details 206
Chapter 35 Toga Party 210
Chapter 36 Breaking the Enemy 220

Magick: archaic spelling of magic.

Careful, the fine line between good and evil is not discernible at first glance.

*Stop fighting yourself and start
fighting for yourself.
The Revolutionary*

ONE

C H A O S

Matilda and George came home from church to find their house engulfed in flames. Andria screamed as she ran out of the house, her hands severely burned.

Andria took off her denim vest, and a box of wooden matches fell from her pocket.

"Where did you get those matches?" asked George.

"Near the fire pit," Andria replied sarcastically. The candles set the living room curtains on fire."

It was difficult for the Clays to adjust to their daughter's growing need for attention. Andria was aware of her ominous side. At night, Matilda and George are frightened by Andria, standing in a trance at the foot of their bed.

Andria's parents were so concerned about the behavior that they sent her to a private boarding school until she was twenty-one years old. Shortly after her twenty seconds birthday, Andria married Francis Cozbi. He was a handsome man with deep brown eyes, a slim build, and an alcoholic. Andria drove him insane with her almond-shaped eyes and thick black hair. She had mastered the art of manipulating her husband to the point where she could get whatever she desired. However, there was a cost. She had to put up with his rage.

Andria had a successful nursing career, but she yearned for more. Francis and Andria welcomed their first child, a daughter, and named her Keira.

The baby had a fever. Her delicate ears were red, and she cried uncontrollably. Francis could not stand the baby's cry anymore, so he slammed the crib against the wall, causing Keira to scream. Andria ran and picked up the baby.

"Shut that kid up. I cannot take it anymore!" He shouted.

"Francis, you son of a bitch! Are you trying to kill her; she's only five days old. The baby needs a doctor," hollered Andria.

Francis left the house and walked to the nearest pub. That night he came home and brutally beat Andria.

Five years later.

Keira's parents argued more often over the years, and the violence escalated. Keira could not take the violence anymore, crept out of the house, and ran to a nearby church. The lights dimmed as she entered the vestibule, creating strange shadows on the old stone walls. Keira shivered as she stood in front of the candlelit tabernacle, praying for an end to the violence. In the morning, all is quiet, as though that horrible night had never happened. Andria remained silent, expecting a repeat of last night's beatings. She pressed against Keira, kissing the top of her head, and Francis sat at the breakfast table without a care in the world.

Another night of fighting between her parents has begun, and Keira seeks refuge at The Nativity Church. Officer Longhouse, patrolling Water Street at two a.m., discovered Keira sitting on the church steps.

"Why are you here in the dead of night?" The officer asked.

Keira shrugged, "I am waiting for the church to open."

"What is your name?"

"Keira," she whispered.

"Is there something you are not telling me?"

"No, sir," she replied.

Keira was frightened of her parents. As she watched her father beat her mother day after day, she feared the same thing. Her mother had fallen into a depression and became easily irritated with Keira.

Keira pleaded with the officer.

"Please, let me go home. I will never do this again."

Keira never returned to the church. By the age of twelve, she had tried suicide. In her twenties, she planned another suicide attempt. As Keira lay in her bed, contemplating her death, a supernatural force surrounded her. It lifted her out of a deep depression.

TWO

DEATH AND DECEPTION

Francis came home drunk and passed out on the couch. Then later that evening, Andria tried to wake him.

"Francis, please wake up, and come to bed."

Andria stared at his sweaty face with disgust.

"I have taken all I can from you, Francis. Your beatings and insults stop now. Die, you drunken psychopath."

Andria grabbed a cushion from under his head and smothered him until he was *dead*. The level of intoxication was a stage five stupor; therefore, there was little resistance. Witnessing her husband's death gave her an ultimate high.

Andria couldn't sleep after what she had done. She thought about wrapping his body in a sheet and burying him in the backyard. Dismemberment would make it easier to bury him in the basement. Even so, his decaying body parts would stink up the house. Andria lived in a community of nosy neighbors, and she was terrified of being caught. Andria had mentally rehearsed all the possible question-and-answer the police would throw at her and mournful facial expressions. Then, at eight o'clock in the morning, she decided to call the police and play the part of the innocent wife who woke up to find her husband dead.

"Mam, what time did your husband come home?" Asked Detective Miller.

"I have no idea. It was around eleven o'clock last night. Francis entered the house, his legs trembling, and flopped on the couch."

"Why didn't you call an ambulance?

"Francis is an alcoholic who often sleeps for days after a drunken binge.

"Andria, you appear indifferent to your husband's death."

Having the ability to cry at will, Andria continued.

"He was an evil man. Karma has a way of making things right."

Dr. Hajji entered the room, bowed his head, and avoided making eye contact. He never speaks unless necessary.

"Francis has been here for a while, suffering from alcohol poisoning. So there is no need for an autopsy."

Before leaving, he stared into Andria's eyes, sending chills down her spine.

"He must have been in a hurry. Dr. Hajji usually checks the corpse's core temperature; sorry; I mean the body before he leaves." Said detective Miller.

THREE

THE LIES BEGIN

Andria was chopping vegetables when she noticed a woman peering through the screen door. She cut her finger on the cleaver, surprised by the unexpected visitor.

"Sorry, Andria, I did not mean to scare you. Are you preparing dinner?" Asked Marion.

"BBQ ribs and granny's caramel apple pie for dessert." She said proudly.

"Marion, come in. Would you like a cup of tea?"

"No thanks. Devon is waiting for me. I'm throwing a party tomorrow night, and you're invited."

"What is the occasion?" Asked Andria.

"Devon's final divorce papers arrived yesterday, and I hoped we could help him celebrate his newfound freedom."

"Excellent, I will call the sitter."

"He is looking forward to reuniting with old friends. Sorry for leaving so soon, but I have some baking to do."

Devon is a successful corporate lawyer, and he is Andria's ticket to a life of luxury.

It's eight o'clock at night, and the babysitter hasn't arrived yet—a black Charger squeals around the corner and grinds to a halt in front of the house. Andria stood on the veranda patiently.

"I'm sorry for being late," Veronica said. "I just got off work."

"Don't worry. I'm thankful you are here. My cell number is on the dining room table if something comes up. Oh, and Keira's bedtime is no later than nine o'clock."

Andria walked into Marion's house wearing a red gown, stiletto heels, and a matching clutch.

"I have known you for at least ten years, and you are still gorgeous, said Devon."

Andria could not take her eyes off him. He was still in decent shape, with a glimmer of gray in his hair.

"You haven't changed all that much."

"Andria, sit next to me, and I'll get you something to drink."

"Please, a chilled Pinot Grigio," said Andria.

"What prompted you to reintroduce wine into your life? Remember that night when we ate spaghetti and drank a cheap bottle of red wine? You were so sick that you vowed never to do it again." Flashbacks of Devon holding back Andria's hair as she hung her head over the toilet bowl flooded her mind.

"My wine preferences have evolved."

"That' s good to hear," he smiled.

Andria had little to say; her eyes fixed on him.

"Andria, what is it? Is there something bothering you?"

"I was thinking about the day you married June. It was the saddest day of my life. I get a little nostalgic seeing you again."

"June had persuaded me that I was not your type. She rarely had a kind word to say about anyone.'

"Devon, do you have children?"

"We tried for a while until I discovered her birth control pills. I could not imagine June, my ex-wife, changing a dirty diaper. When Marion told me that she had invited you to the party, I asked her not to invite anyone else."

"Devon, no one else is coming?"

"No. I hope you are not disappointed?"

"Not at all. I was hoping to have you all to myself."

"Sneaky, aren't you?"

"There are times when it is necessary."

"Marion said you were a widow."

"His drinking had finally killed him. Let's not talk about him right now. The sun is rising, and I would like to get back before Keira wakes up. Come to dinner tonight and meet my daughter.

Devon arrived at Andria's just as the Italian lasagna came out of the oven.

Before we sit for dinner, I have something to tell you. Andria, you should know that I am a sorcerer."

"What does this have to do with me?"

"If we are to be in a relationship, I intend to be completely honest about my life."

"Devon, will I be cursed if we see one another? Witchcraft is not my cup of tea."

Keira dashed into the room as if someone was chasing her.

"I was going to kiss you," Devon whispered.

"I can't find Buddy. I searched everywhere." Said Keira.

"Keira, this is Devon."

"Are you my mother's boyfriend?" she asked.

"Don't be rude, Keira," Andria warned.

"It's fine; she's just curious. How would you feel about that?"

Keira sighed and shrugged her shoulders. "Sure, as long as you don't hurt my mother."

"Andria, did your husband beat you?" Asked Devon.

"It is over now. Francis will never hurt us again."

"Keira, I hear barking in the kitchen," he said.

Keira ran off to stop Buddy from eating her snacks. Buddy jumped up on a chair, climbed onto the table, and helped himself to a few banana muffins.

Andria realized she had strained their relationship by casting doubt on his way of life. Her plans would have failed if she hadn't approved his magickal work.

"Andria, I am descended from a long line of witches. If you can't accept who I am, this relationship will fail."

Andria hugged him to show her support.

"Do whatever you want; this has nothing to do with us. It's my turn to be transparent. Keira began giggling in the middle of the night when she was three months old. I entered her room, and there she was, hovering over the crib. Keira remained motionless after I placed an enchanted fabric on her bassinet."

"Where did you find something like that?" Asked Devon

"I met a lady at the village café, and she knew of Keira's abilities. She gave me the fabric and showed me how to drape it over Keira's crib.

"Do you still have this cloth?"

"Yes, it is hidden in my closet. Give me a minute, and I will get it for you."

The enchanted material was thrown on the bed and transformed into a field of energy.

"I have never seen anything like it before. Your daughter has a unique destiny."

"My daughter is not all that special," said Andria spitefully.

"How can you say that Keira is not gifted?"

Andria found it odd that he had become fond of her daughter early in their relationship.

You seem overly interested in my daughter. You're not one of those people who have an interest in children? Are you?

"That is revolting. Andria, you do not understand. My interests for Keira are honorable."

"Let's not talk about it anymore," said Andria.

Devon decided to end his visit due to Andria's lousy attitude.

"It's late. I have a court appearance tomorrow morning."

"Please do not leave. I apologized for my bad behavior."

"What brings you to the courthouse? Is something going on?"

"I'm a lawyer. If everything goes as planned, I intend to run for mayor next year."

"Wonderful, I'll vote for you," said Andria.

"What have you been up to all these years?" Asked Devon.

"I worked in healthcare before Keira was born. It was difficult to shift from a promising career to motherhood."

"Andria, I cannot make up for all the years you have suffered, but I would like to take you out for a special dinner. How about tomorrow evening? Let's say around seven?"

"I will be waiting," Andria replied.

Andria expected Devon to hold her, but she quickly realized that expressing affection was not Devon's nature. Andria was tolerant of his way. She preferred money over sentiment.

They arrived at Rose Garden Inn, and in a debonaire sort of way, he threw his keys to the parking attendant.

"This place is high-end," said Andria.

"Price is not a concern. Order anything you want."

Devon picked up the room key he had reserved before dinner. Andria opened the door and stepped into a luxurious suite. There was champagne on ice on the breakfast table and a black velvet box on a white satin pillow.

"Devon, what is this?"

She picked up a jewelry box from the satin pillow. Devon whispered as he kissed her lips.

"I promise that you will not want for anything if you marry me."

He placed the diamond necklace around Andria's neck and the matching engagement ring on her finger.

"This diamond is enormous!"

"A ten-carat diamond for my future wife." He said.

"I have waited a long time for this moment." Andria thought.

"Keira will carry my last name. I have taken the liberty of preparing the documents myself. All I need is your signature," Devon said.

"Why are you so fixated on my daughter?"

"When we marry, Keira will become my daughter."

Andria knew that her true colors were beginning to show.

"I have been a single mom for eight years and am overprotective for good reasons."

"Of course, she will always be an important part of our lives, and I understand that having someone new in your life can be difficult. You have probably noticed that I have difficulty expressing myself. I was born into a conservative family. I express my love by providing you with a lovely home and money. I hoped you could sense how much I adored you both without saying anything."

Devon woke up the following day, expecting to see Andria lying beside him.

"Andria, please come here. Your future husband will show you what is in store for you first thing in the morning."

"We'll have plenty of time for that later. I'm planning a menu for our engagement dinner. Invite your business partners and their wives," said Andria.

"The engagement party is not necessary."

"It is tradition. Our friends and family come together to remember dumb things we did when we were single and toast our upcoming nuptials."

Three weeks later, family and guests arrive at the Rose Garden Inn. Andria had reserved a private dining room with an open bar. Devon stood at the door, relieved to see his business partners show up on such short notice.

"Andrew, Pierce, thanks for coming. I know it was a little sudden."

"I wasn't sure we'd make it, but Libby offered to rearrange my schedule," Pierce explained.

Devon piqued Libby's interest. She kissed him on the lips, leaving a smear of red lip gloss around his mouth.

"Devon, wipe that off before Andria sees it." Said Pierce, giving Devon a handkerchief.

"Devon, your impending marriage surprised me. We will no longer be able to use him to make our husbands insanely jealous, Ivy." Said Libby.

Ivy, a woman of great wisdom, abruptly interjected. "Devon, ignore that woman's lies."

"Devon chuckled. "Libby got drunk last Christmas and pinned me against the stove, trying to remove my pants."

"That's right, I remember," said Andrew. "Devon, you desperately called out for Pearce, and Libby had no memory of it the following day.

"Devon, now that everyone knows your secrets, how is life treating you?" Asked Ivy.

"Keira, Andria's daughter, has embraced our union with open arms."

"I am happy for you, but have you forgotten? Your ex-wife turned out to be a thorn in your side and took a hefty sum of money when she left. Whatever you decide to do, I will support you. Are you sure about Andria?"

"Ivy, I am as confident as I can be. We have known each other for a long time."

"It has been a while since you have seen each other. You managed to get out of your last marriage without losing your shirt. Research is always a good idea," said Ivy.

Devon grew wary of Ivy because she is one of his most trusted friends, who is usually right.

"If I have to investigate my future wife, I might as well cancel the wedding. However, I do have a little something up my sleeve. There is no harm in being practical."

"Devon Wolf, I have always known you were a genius," Ivy whispered.

Ivy joined Andria at the bar and ordered another Baileys.

"Andria, what a lovely name. I have been around for a long time, and even though you have not asked for my advice, I will still give it to you. Marriage is about love, trust, and selflessness. It is not about money. On the other hand, deception leads to dissatisfaction, greed, and poverty.

Andria sighed, "Ivy, what gives you the right to speak to me that way? I am not one of your kids. Thanks for the lecture, and you are right; I did not ask for your help. Mind your own business, witch."

Andria returned to Devon's table, fearful that this astute lady would discover Andria's deception.

"Ivy is talkative tonight. What was that about?"

"It's nothing. Ivy gives me the creeps." Said Andria.

FOUR

WEDDING DAY BLUES

"Marion, where are my pearls? I have an hour until the ceremony begins."

"Relax, or you're going to be a nervous wreck by the time you get to the altar."

Devon walked into the room, holding a document.

"Out, you can't see the bride before the wedding; it's bad luck," Marion shouted.

Devon ignored his sister's scolding.

"Andria, I need you to sign this prenuptial agreement."

"Are you serious? We love each other. What if I refuse?" Said Andria.

"I will have no alternative but to postpone the wedding."

"Devon, please give me the bloody contract."

Andria resentfully signed the papers and threw them back at him.

"I hope you're happy."

"What a fool I've been all these years. It's all about money. Is that right, Andria?"

Devon left the room before Andria could answer with one of her excuses, slamming the door behind him.

Slowly walking to the altar, Andria was still visibly upset and knew that a change of strategy would be in order. The money and prestige that Andria would have had if Devon were to leave disappeared when she signed the prenuptial.

The wedding went off without a hitch. The newlyweds dashed to their wedding suite to change their clothes shortly after the ceremony. Their emotional distance was a reliable predictor of what would happen in the future.

"Devon, signing those documents made me feel like an outsider, someone you can't trust. I'm your wife, for heaven's sake."

"I didn't have a choice, Andria. My business partners insisted on a prenuptial agreement, or I would be forced to leave the company. Don't worry; you will live in luxury after I die. But you get nothing if you leave me."

She tried to persuade him of her innocence. But she was not convincing.

"Devon, it's not all about the money."

"You have made your case. Take that innocent look off your face. I see right through it. The prenuptial protects both of us. We were married to other people in the past, and know-how quickly, love can sour."

Andria took off her wedding gown and stood naked in front of him. Devon gently kissed her neck, but he could not get into the moment. All he could think about were Ivy's words of wisdom. Andria pushed Devon onto the bed and took off his trousers. But Devon is in no mood to play. Andria's anger at having to sign the prenuptial revealed the depth of her love and what she wanted, Devon's money.

Andria's attempt to arouse him had failed.

"I'm sorry, Andria; this is not the time. Said Devon.

Insulted, Andria continued. "Is it my technique?"

"You don't understand what you have done to me," said Devon.

Andria went on. "Where do we go from here? I hope you're not thinking of an annulment or divorce; I'll contest it."

Devon stifled a sigh. "How could I have been so wrong about you?"

Although heartbroken, he did love Andria despite her selfish nature.

"Tomorrow, we are all going for a drive. You won't be disappointed."

"Give me a hint," said Andria.

"No spoilers. Who knows, maybe we can save this marriage."

"Are you still in love with me despite everything? True, I enjoy money, but I still care about you." Said Andria.

"Love is much more than caring," said Devon.

The newlyweds returned to the banquet hall. Andrew drank more than he intended, asking Andria to dance.

"Devon, do you mind?" Asked Andria.

"Go ahead. We were supposed to have the first dance at our wedding. I guess that is not going to happen."

Devon walked around the reception hall and expressed his gratitude to his guest for being part of the wedding. He felt a slight tug on his jacket. "Daddy," yawn, "when are we going home?"

Devon glanced at his watch. "It's one-thirty in the morning; no wonder you're tired. We have to pull your mother off that dance floor."

Devon walked over to the microphone, and the music stopped. He thanked his guest for making their special day a success and announced that he had a little one to tuck into bed. Andria slipped her lace shawl over her shoulders and complained about not partying through the night with her friends.

They drove to Virginia Beach the next day, where a new building was being built on seven acres of lush green land.

"I'm sorry, Devon, Keira was feeling off this morning and refused to come along," Andria explained.

"Poor kid, she must be overtired." Devon Murmured.

Devon knew deep down that Andria did not want Keira around.

"When will this house be ready?"

"Not for a while. The limestone and other materials haven't arrived yet. Construction on this Gothic castle began a few months ago, and actually, they're behind schedule."

"Testy, aren't we? Soon, I hope." Said Andria.

"I'm sure it would improve where we currently live." Andria moaned.

"I'll rent out the old place when our new house is finished." "Does that satisfy you?" Devon frowned.

Her negativity is getting on his nerves.

"Why don't you cast a spell to finish the house sooner?" She chuckled.

"Oh, shut up, Andria." Devon snapped.

They arrived home late that evening to police searching their home.

"What's going on?" Asked Devon.

"Mr. Wolf, I'm Inspector Paolone. Veronica reported someone breaking into the house. The intruder entered the house through your daughter's bedroom window."

Andria gasped. "Is Keira okay?"

Inspector Paolone took off his hat and continued. "Your daughter is fine, but I can't say the same for that man. The alarm must have startled him; he fell from the window and broke his neck."

"Detective, you look troubled," Devon uttered.

"Mr. Wolf, we measured the distance from the window to the ground, and it was less than five feet in height. Have you ever heard of a fatal injury of this kind?" Asked the Inspector.

"I'm sure it is possible. What are you suggesting?" Asked Andria.

"Mrs. Wolf, his neck appears to have been broken before the fall."

Andria spoke tersely. "Surely, you're not suspecting Keira or Veronica of murdering this man? As for Devon and I, we have been on the interstate for the last two hours."

"Mrs. Wolf, whoever killed this man, had enormous strength. According to the coroner, if more force were applied, we'd be looking at a headless body."

Devon lifted the sheet covering the dead man's face.

Andria screamed. "Impossible; Francis died eight years ago and was cremated.

Devon continued. "Detective, we needed to apply for Francis' death certificate to get our marriage license.

The detective continues. "More mysterious is that this man did not have a once of blood remaining in his body."

"We will conduct a thorough investigation, and if anything else comes up, we will be in touch," said Detective Paolone.

"I would like to see my daughter, said Andria."

"Of course, Mrs. Wolf, we are done here."

"Keira, are you okay." Asked Devon.

Keira looked into his eyes and said, "He was already dead?"

Devon shivered as the words came out of her mouth.

"Keira, did you know that man?" Asked Devon.

"My old dad was not supposed to scare us that way," Keira whispered.

Devon turned his attention to Veronica. "What happened?"

"Mr. Wolf, a man, opened the window and entered the room. I grabbed Keira, ran into the bathroom, and dialed 911. We heard an animal howl, and someone fell to the floor, said Ronnie.

"Well, this is convenient. No one has seen anything," Andria said.

The ambulance arrived at the hospital and placed the body bag on the coroner's examination table. Dr. Hajji unzipped the human remains pouch and discovered a mixture of black earth and ash. "Perfect," said the coroner.

Later that night, Andria rushed to the bathroom with her hand covering her mouth. Keira knocks frantically on the door.

"Mom, are you all right. Open the door, please."

"I'm okay. We're going to have a new addition to our family

"Mom, you're pregnant?" Asked Keira.

"I've had morning sickness for a while."

"Are you sure, Andria?" Devon asked softly.

Andria continued, "yes, I'm sure. I've noticed subtle changes to my body."

"Like what," asked Keira.

"Other than morning sickness, weight gain, and an aversion to certain foods. I must be at least five or six months pregnant. I'm so thin it barely shows." said Andria.

Devon could not contain his enthusiasm. He announced the baby's expected arrival to anyone who would listen.

Several months later, Andria is in labor at three thirty-three in the morning. In time, Devon drove to the hospital to welcome his little boy into the world.

"What should we call him?" Asked Devon.

Andria smiled. "Matthew, after your father."

"Matthew is an excellent name. My dad was a gentleman and caring man when nobody was watching," said Devon.

"I like Matthew; let's go with that," Andria whispered.

"His name will be Devon, Matthew Wolf."

Andria chuckled. "I knew your name would fit in somewhere."

"That's a given, said Devon."

Four Years Later. - Matthew is a happy little boy who loves to play with marbles and a toy fire truck his dad gave him for Christmas. For the last few weeks, Devon wakes up in the morning to find his son curled up in the small of his back.

"Hey, little man, did you know you are our ray of sunshine?" Said Devon.

Matthew jumped out of bed, and his infectious laughter filled the house. He ran into the kitchen and saw his mother crack three eggs in a mixing bowl.

"Can I help?" Asked Matthew."

"No, sweetie. I'm good for now. Next week, you are going to be five years old. What's your favorite cake?" Asked Andria.

Matthew jumped up and down around the kitchen table. "Chocolate, with red fire truck icing."

Andria held Matthew in her arms. "Of course, you can have whatever you want."

"Mom, don't forget to make some licorice marbles for my cake."

Andria giggled. "Licorice marbles? You are very creative for your age."

"Mommy, last night, I saw a blue lady in my room. She said that it was time to go home soon. This is my home, right?"

"Yes, Matthew, this is your home. It was just a dream." Said Andria.

Matthew shrugged his shoulders, smiled, and ran outside with a pocket full of marbles.

Keira walked into the kitchen and stuck her figure into the cake batter.

"Stop doing that, Keira Wolf; I'm baking your brother's birthday cake. I thought you had left for the library." Said Andria.

"Don't worry about it, mom; usually, you don't care where I am. Matthew's birthday is next week; it's a little early for his cake, isn't it?"

"I'm going to bake the cake ahead of time and put it in the freezer. Should something come up, all I have to do is add the icing and decorations."

"Where's Matthew now?" Asked Keira. "There are a few crafts that I would like to teach him."

"Never mind your witchy stuff; you create such a mess. Make yourself useful and take Matthew to the park."

"Really, mother, there's nothing witchy about using branches and leaves to create a bird's nest."

Matthew loves this park. Artists come here to entertain people of all ages. Some artists are homeless and accept coins if you have any to spare. Matthew ran to his favorite booth. This older man has been a face painter for fifty years, and today is his ninetieth birthday.

"Your back, master Matthew. What will it be today?" The man asked.

"Mr. Ellis, we would like a yellow and blue butterfly painted on our faces," said Matthew.

"And who's this beautiful young lady?" he asked.

"This is Keira, my bestess sister in the whole world."

Keira tried to correct her little brother's English.

"Matthew, the word you are looking for is best and not bestess."

Matthew countered. "No, Keira, bestess is bigger than best."

Keira's heart melted. "Okay, sport, you win; let's get our faces painted."

Keira and Matthew walked around the park and ran into a food vendor selling foot-long hot dogs.

"I want one of those longdogs," said Matthew.

"Matthew, they're called a foot-long hot dog," said Keira.

Matthew was sure Keira was wrong. "No, no, no, Keira. There called longdog. When the longdogs aren't hot, the man gives them to me. So, if the longdog were hot, it would burn my teefs, and I'd call them hot longdogs."

"Okay," said Keira. Matthew, as long as you know what you're talking about, that matters. Look at the size of that sausage. It's massive. We'll each have half," said Keira.

They sat by a pond, eating their hot dog, and watched the ducklings swimming with their mother.

"Keira, I saw a blue lady last night, and she told me I was coming home soon. I got scared and ran into daddy's room."

"Matthew, I'm sure it was just a bad dream."

"That's what mommy said. But I know it was for real."

FIVE

THE BLUE LADY HAS COME

Keira was on her way home from school when she heard the sirens. She walked into the house and found Nana sitting near the fireplace.

"I'm sorry, Keira, he's gone."

"Who are you talking about, Nana?"

"Matthew was sitting on the sidewalk, playing with his marbles. A driver missed his turn and hit him."

Matthew was only four years old, and he was the victim of a speeding drunk driver. Several days later, yellow roses were carefully arranged around the memorial room. There were three yellow marbles in Matthew's folded hands and a large blue rose without thorns. Devon heard someone whispering.

"I've heard that roses help mask the smell of decay."

Devon walked over to the man and said, "Do you mind; I don't need to hear your disparaging remarks."

Keira saw her family standing around Matthew's casket and sitting near the exit. A man rocked back and forth, whispering, "I'm sorry. What have I done!"

She walked over and placed her arms around him, aware that he was responsible for Matthew's death. He broke away from Keira's arms and ran out the door. An angel made of granite fell from the funeral home's rooftop and crushed him. Keira saw the incident and didn't feel a thing.

"His torment is over," said Keira.

Andria kissed Matthew's forehead, "goodbye, my little man. Mommy will see you soon."

Devon placed a twenty-four-carat gold nickel in his shirt pocket to celebrate his fifth birthday. It's Keira's turn to say goodbye. Her lips touched his cold brow, and she began to cry. The reality of Matthew's death had finally registered.

The pallbearers lowered Matthew's small white casket to the ground. Andria rushed to stop them and pleaded, "No, please, that's my baby. You can't do this."

Devon held Andria in his arms, and together they wept bitterly.

It was a long ride home, and emotionally, everyone was drained.

Keira was the first person to enter the house. "Dad, it's like the house knows someone's missing."

"Keira, every house has its own life."

During the night, mournful cries echoed through the home. The following morning, Keira walked into the living room and stood by the window.

"The earth is a never-ending hell. "With all this misery, why would anyone want to come here?"

Andria stayed up late that night knitting Matthew's sweater, which she had planned to give him for his birthday. Devon stared into the fireplace, numb and perplexed.

As the full moon shone through the blinds, Keira lay in her bed, tossing and turning. An electrical current passed through her body. Startled, Keira jumped out of bed. Books flew through the air, and she was thrown to the ground by a strong gust of wind. Andria burst into the room, shocked to see the chaos. Keira rose to her feet as if she had an iron bar running down her spine. "No, she cried out, raising both hands. At that moment, all activity ceased.

"Mom, what happened?"

"Keira, you are responsible for what happened here tonight."

"How is it my fault?"

"Keira, keep your emotions under control, or you'll kill someone one day. I don't know where your gifts came from."

"What is going on.?" Asked Keira.

"Losing your brother must have been the catalyst that triggered this turmoil. A couple of months after you were born, I met a lady at the restaurant, and we sat down together. She helped me understand your gifts."

"Mom, who sent her?" Asked Keira.

"She never said, and I didn't ask. You hovered over your crib, and I had to attach a special net over your bed to protect you. My biggest fear was that you would fly out of the window. You immediately returned to the crib. This mysterious lady instructed me to raise my hands and say Nikhil, the word no in Latin."

"Mom, if you and dad aren't like me, am I adopted?"

Timidly, Andria replied. "Francis and I flew to Egypt for our honeymoon. One night, I suffered from severe abdominal pains and vomited several times until morning. Your dad and I drove to the hospital, and we found out that I was pregnant."

Andria wasn't ready to tell Keira who her paternal father was. She had a weird experience that was difficult to believe. Andria fell into a deep sleep one night and dreamt of wild roses, as far as the eye could see. A stranger stood before her, wearing nothing but droplets of moisture running down his muscular body. He took Andria into his arms and laid her down on a soft bed of rosebuds. At his touch, she trembled, wanting more of him.

"Who are you?" Andria whispered.

The stranger said nothing. He removed the lace ties on her gown until her silky skin was exposed. Intuitively, she knew this strange being would not hurt her. He loved her like no other man ever had.

He whispered, "Andria, our daughter, may not have my nature, but she will inherit my powers. This child will have an important decision to make. Will she walk into the light or serve the darkness?"

"Who are you?" Andria insisted.

"My name is Chrysalis, and I serve all that is evil. Our daughter will join us when the time is right."

Andria sat on Keira's bed with her eyes closed, remembering the experience.

"Mom, is there something you're not telling me?"

Andria composed herself. "You worry too much. Get some sleep, and we will talk again in the morning."

SIX

THE GUARDIAN

"I'm freezing. Why do we stay in this old house?" asked Keira.

Devon sighed. "I was born here, and it will be restored to its original state one day. You will have to put up with it until our new home is ready. I've already told you this. Do I have to repeat myself?"

Keira knew better than to keep on gripping.

"Get ready for bed if you are that cold."

The lights were still on in her father's den, and as always, Keira was looking for an adventure. She took the opportunity to look around his office without asking permission. She sat at Devon's desk, amazed by the intricate works of ancient Egyptian hieroglyphs.

"Hey, Dad, why are you studying a book on Forbidden Black Magick?"

"Research! Keira, leave my office and go to your room. Your uncle Matteo is visiting, and I don't want to hear a peep from you." Devon said anxiously.

At the mention of his name Keira froze.

"If dad knew how Matteo tried to touch me every time he visited, he would kill him." Keira thought.

Keira dashed to her room, picking up a vintage letter opener from the desk.

Keira lay in her bed, listening as her parents laughed with Matteo. Keira dozed off and began to dream of a beast chasing her. Keira could feel the creature's hot breath on her neck. He was desperately trying to stop her.

He spoke with a familiar voice. "Wait for me."

When Keira heard his massive paws hit the ground, she knew she couldn't outrun him. She stopped and turned to face the enemy. Her piercing blue eyes shone brightly like the sun. In surrender, the creature lay on the ground and said,

"Ego custodem."

"Are you my guardian? Who sent you?"

Keira woke up from her dream with the sudden screeching sound of the bedroom door opening. Except for a nightlight plugged into the wall, the room was pitch black.

Keira saw a silhouette standing near the door. She was terrified and could feel her heart pounding in her ears. As he approached the bed, a rough, calloused hand crawled up her leg. Keira had a strong sense of impending death.

"No, get away from me," Keira screamed as she kicked her legs up and down. Again, Keira screamed and called out for her parents, but there was no answer. Keira is terrified, and she feels helpless in this cretin's hands.

"Your mom and dad are out for the evening, and I'm your sitter. So, shut up, bitch."

Something broke inside her at that precise moment. She'd lost a piece of herself. Will Keira ever be whole again? As Keira struggled under the weight of his body, he continued his disgusting attempt to touch her. She grabbed the letter opener from under her pillow and stabbed into the darkness, hoping to stop him. An unknown force snatched the brass letter opener from her hand, and a warm spray of blood covered her face. Keira heard a thump on the floor. All of Keira's fear and panic had left her.

She swung her cold bare feet over to the side of the bed and landed in a warm puddle of sticky liquid. She fumbles, looking for her bedside lamp. The light exposed a horrific scene. Keira walked over to Matteo, lying on the floor with a letter opener firmly fixed into his neck. Keira was fascinated by the sensation of warm blood between her toes and watched as he took his last breath. Keira was not upset by what she had witnessed and ran to take a shower, leaving a trail of bloody footprints behind her.

Keira's parents arrived home late and found their daughter reading on the couch.

"What are you doing out of bed?" Asked Devon.

Keira responded with a mocking smile on her face.

"Matteo is resting in my bedroom."

"Matteo? He was told to check the windows and leave the house." Said Andria.

"He doesn't look good." Said Keira.

Taken back by Keira's response, they rushed to her room. They saw Matteo on the floor in a pool of blood and a brass letter opener firmly embedded into his throat.

Devon felt nauseous, and Andria felt faint in his arms. He led her to the kitchen and sat her at the table.

"Midnight snack? I'm your sous-chef for the evening. I'm starving to death." Said Keira.

Angrily, her father asked. "What the hell happened here tonight?"

Her father's anger does not change Keira's mood.

"Matteo wanted a piece of me; I said no, but he wouldn't listen. My guardian was the one who murdered him."

Keira continued to cook as if nothing had happened.

"Mom, have some bacon with me. I've cooked enough to feed a sounder of wild boar."

Devon continued. "Who is this guardian?"

"Perhaps he's the hellhound I have dreamt about," Keira replied.

Perplexed by her daughter's behavior, Andria persisted.

"Honey, are you ok? Tell us what happened."

"I took the letter opener from dad's desk when I heard Matteo was in the house. Matteo came to my room, and he was all over me. I tried to stab Matteo, but someone took the brass letter opener out of my hand. That's it. I didn't see anything else. There is no need for all these questions; someone else killed him."

"He tried to touch me while your backs were turned. I tried to warn you about Matteo and his dirty habits, but you usually shrugged me off. Death is too good for this guy."

Outraged, Devon continued. "Andria, did Matteo come after our daughter?"

"Damn it, Devon, that's not important right now. I'm worried about going to prison because of this misfit's actions. Devon, something is wrong with Keira; I'm calling the police."

"Your concern for Keira's well-being. is disgusting." Devon uttered.

As Andria dialed the emergency number, Devon took her cell phone and smashed it against the wall.

"You idiot! The only person you care about is you! My political career will be over if anyone finds out what happened here tonight. Contenders for the mayor's seat are waiting for a scandal of this magnitude to destroy everything I have worked for all these years."

Surprised by his response, Andria shouted. "Devon, a man has died in our home. Becoming the Mayor can wait? Your daughter has not shown the slightest remorse for Matteo's death."

"Why would she have remorse? The man tried to rape her. What's wrong with you, Andria?"

"Are you suggesting that we cover up the murder?"

"My life will be over when the public learns that our daughter murdered a man. Keira will be locked up in an asylum forever."

Devon composed himself before his temper got out of hand.

"Andria, there's something you should see." Said Devon.

"I know all about her witchy powers. She can fly, change the weather, and whatever else she can dream up."

Andria walked over to the dining room table and sat in a captain's chair.

Keira began to levitate, drifting gracefully through the house. She stretched out her hands toward her mother, and they were both suspended in midair. Andria became anxious and ordered Keira to put her down.

Shaken up by this experience, Andria feared that Keira's abilities would be used against her.

"I was aware of the levitation, but to fly around the room with another person is amazing. Leave us; your dad and I have some business to discuss."

"Business?" Said Devon.

Andria told Devon about Keira's biological father. Andria couldn't keep the secret any longer. Despite the lies, she hoped he would believe her. Andria would not be troubled if Devon decided to leave. She would receive a large settlement.

"You've forgotten about my involvement with the paranormal. I don't care about your past. It happened before we met. Andria, you knew what was going on. After all, your union produced a gifted child. You have tasted the nectar of shadows. In the beginning, you were afraid of being cursed due to my involvement in the dark arts. You should have pushed the demon away, but instead, you cursed yourself. You will yearn for him until the end of your days."

Andria watched Keira pouring the bacon fat into an old soup can.

"Devon, this is not your daughter," said Andria.

He held Keira's hand, "you're wrong. I dried her tears, and I was by her side when she was sick.

"Keira is a teenager, and she has exposed her dark side. There is help for her. We have to tell someone. She will be drugged and sent to an asylum when necessary. Otherwise, this may happen again." Said Andria.

"Andria, are you trying to get rid of her again?"

Andria said nothing. Devon's face became dark, and his eyes menacing. He wrapped his fingers around her necklace. "I am through with your lousy attitude. Matteo's death will be our secret."

Still holding on to her pearls, Devon dragged Andria to the kitchen window, and they both observed the wind gusting through the lush green forest a short distance from their home.

Devon yanked Andria's pearls off her neck.

"You know I'm not a betting man, but I would wager that there are bodies dumped in those woods from time to time."

Andria watched her precious pearls bouncing across the floor and said, "I'll keep my mouth shut."

Devon gazed into Keira's beautiful blue eyes, and for the first time, he saw life.

"Dad, I did not kill Matteo."

"You are unique, Keira. I believe that an unknown force is protecting you."

"Andria, perhaps it's for the best. Matteo had no business putting his hands on my little girl. Keira's defender saved me the trouble of killing him. I will take care of the body; you clean up the mess."

Devon hid the body in the forest where the wolves gathered, and this night was never spoken of again.

SEVEN

L O O K I N G
F O R   D I R T

"Here is the new constituents list that you requested. Our last fundraiser was a success. According to our door-to-door promotion, your popularity has grown. I must say, Devon, keep this up, and soon you will be Mayor of Virginia Beach."

"Lance, how far back are the other candidates." Asked Devon.

"Sir, Margo is your close second, and Tom Wallis is third."

"That's excellent news. I needed to hear that today. We are going to keep the momentum going. Please get my private Jet ready. It's leaving for England early in the morning."

"Mr. Wolf, are you aware that you have meetings this evening that may extend into the late hours?"

"Lance, you are watching over me as my mom did."

"Sir. I am just trying to keep you organized and on time."

"Are you sure there is no other reason?" Asked Devon.

"I know my place. You are married, and I respect you for the man you are. But if you change your mind, you have my number." Said Lance.

"Don't hold your breath. Let's get back to business. I am not going anywhere. My wife and daughter will be leaving for six weeks."

Just as Lance walked out of the office, Andria entered. Andria glanced around the office with cold resolve, poking fun at the décor. Devon's pride and joy are old abstracts of mystical dragons dating to the eighteenth century. Two black leather wingback chairs that have seen better days sat in front of a large picture window overlooking a beautifully landscaped garden.

"Devon, when are you planning to renovate this place? There should be masterpieces of Sandro Botticelli or Claude Monet hanging on your walls. Your paintings are juvenile. Show a little class, love."

Devon gave Andria a nasty look. He had hoped one of his dragons would fly out of the paintings and skim her derriere with fiery darts.

"Devon, please understand what happened last night; it is more than I can put up with." you make things right, or I will make your life miserable. This year, I'm planning to stay in Paris a little longer."

"You could travel around the world several times a year without breaking the bank with the generous allowance I provide you. However, extra bank withdrawals require my signature."

"Of course, you had me sign a damn prenuptial agreement just before the wedding. The Church overflowed with people hoping for a fairy-tale wedding."

"Andria, why are you so greedy? I have given you everything. Can your lovers do the same?"

"How did you find out about my lovers?"

"Let's not speak of it here; wait until we get home. By the way, you are leaving for England with Keira in the morning."

"England? Hell no. It's a joke, right? Are you sending us to your sister's old villa? That woman is a weird one. On

New Year's Eve, she had a séance and invited your dead relatives to the party." Said Andria scornfully.

Devon laughed. "My sister is a little eccentric, but she means well. I cannot afford a slip of the tongue about what happened with Matteo. Go home, Andria, and we will talk more about this before you leave."

Andria shouted. "Dreams-on. I am not going to England."

Devon roared into the intercom, "Lance, re-schedule my appointment; something has come up.

Devon closed up for the night when Lance's voice came through the intercom one more time.

"Sir, Mr. Wallis is here to see you."

"For crying out loud, I am on my way out. Send him in."

Tom Wallis entered the office, a heavy-set balding man puffing on his imported cigar.

"Devon, I see you are climbing the polls, and soon we will be neck to neck. Is that the reason for your foul mood?

"I'm winning this one, my friend! But it will be a tight race."

Tom took a handkerchief from his shirt pocket, wiped his sweaty head, and replied with a chuckle.

"See this head of mine, the day you win this election is the day I will have grown a full crown of hair. Andria flew past me in the hall, and if looks could kill, everyone would be in front of a firing squad. I overheard her asking the receptionist for directions to the police station. Is everything all right?"

"Nothing to worry about, Wallis. Andria never drove there on her own and had no reason to memorize the route. She must be planning another bake sale to help pay for the new police uniforms. Last year we put on a Halloween ball to help with the cost of new appliances in the cafeteria."

"How come I never heard about your altruism?" Asked Tom.

"I prefer to remain as a private donor. There is no need to brag unless you were looking for an extra vote."

Tom was looking for information to muddy the waters on Election Day.

Tom's eyes narrowed as he gazed into Devon's face.

"Devon, you look worn out."

"A little tired, that's all. Once the election is over, I will join my family in England for a well-deserved vacation. After all, the Mayor should have a little time off. The real truth is, you do not give a damn about my health. Whether I am dead or alive, winning the election is the only thing that matters. Right, Tom?"

Both men smirked, shook hands, and parted.

Devon entered his home, slammed the door, and threw his briefcase on the couch.

"Andria, Keira, please come to the sitting room. We have something to discuss."

"What is going on now, Devon," said Andria."

"Listen to me. I am so close to winning the election. Keira, your aunt Marion is expecting you by the end of this week."

Keira jumped into her father's arms. "Aunt Marion's? I can't wait to see her."

"Keira, you know how to bring out the best in your old dad."

"At least one of us can!" Said Andria,

"Andria, if England is out of the question, leave the country for a couple of weeks. By then, the elections will be over. Wallis is digging up dirt on us. He will go to great lengths to destroy me." Devon uttered.

"How can someone be so cruel?" Asked Keira.

"Keira, everything will be okay."

"Andria, have you decided where you will be going?"

"Devon, no one will ever suspect that I am enjoying the comforts of my own home."

"Have you gone to the police yet? I wouldn't bother; Matteo's body has vanished." Said Devon.

EIGHT

TO CLOSE FOR COMFORT

"Devon, I told you everything about how I met Keira's father, said Andria.

Devon did not want to hear any more about Andria's past. In his opinion, she was a lost cause.

"Stop it; your life before we met is none of my business. Andria, I received a call late last night from Lance. Tom Wallis was found dead and slumped over his desk. Andria, his gold pen, was driven into his neck."

"Devon, do you believe Keira had anything to do with this?"

"There are disturbing parallels to Matteo's death." If anyone discovers Keira's abilities, they will blame her for Tom's death. I'm terrified of taking her out in public. What if she is not able to control her gifts? Keira requires a mentor to teach her how to control her powers." Said Devon.

Andria shouted. "Keira needs to be locked up."

"You keep talking that way; I will put you in a prison of your making, six feet under," Devon whispered.

"We must deal with it. We wouldn't be in this mess if you listened to me when Matteo died." Keira requires a sedative to remove her powers. "I feel safer when her kind isn't around."

"You keep talking about Keira like she's a vicious animal."

Keira walked into the kitchen, hurt and feeling unwanted.

"Dad, do you honestly believe that I can be a threat to our livelihood? Mom, you are a real piece of work. All this time. I thought you accepted me for who I was." Keira paused. "What was the descriptive term you used? Ah, yes, her kind!"

Devon's heart sank when he saw the pain in Keira's eyes.

"No, Keira, I don't see you that way. But others will if we are not careful. I didn't mean it the way it sounded. You must understand that our lavish lifestyle has been due to hard work. The elections will be over by seven o'clock tonight. Nothing must come out until then." Said Devon.

"The answer to your humiliation is to get rid of me. I'm not a dog that you can drug into submission. Your ignorance is the cause of your fears. Dad, you must have a book in that vast library that explains "My Kind." No matter what happens, I am still Keira, your daughter who loves you. Do not bother looking for my kind; I will find them on my own."

Margo Flemings was elected mayor of Virginia Beach in a close election.

"Devon, you were a tough competitor. Margo remarked, "you had me on the edge of my seat."

Devon smiled through the disappointment.

"Margo, you are a visionary, and I wish you the best."

Later that night, Keira began packing her duffle bag.

"Where are you going now?"

"Wherever I am wanted."

"Keira, don't be so naïve. Being homeless is a hard life."

Andria grabbed Keira's arm and sat her down on the bed.

"Before you go off on one of your temper tantrums, listen to me. There are dark forces that will come after you. You will need protection."

Keira slung her duffle bag over her shoulder and walked out the door, ignoring her mother's warning.

"Why should you care? You have made it quite clear how much you love me. I'll deal with it."

Searching for a haven was not easy. Keira walked for several hours until sundown. It's getting late, and she must find a place to sleep. Keira hid in an abandoned apartment building or bus terminal for shelter on rainy days.

Keira stood outside the shopping mall, asking for spare change, when a distinguished-looking man invited her to have dinner. He had a pleasant personality and a diamond wedding band on his left hand. He brought Keira to a fine restaurant and ordered two steak dinners and a large bottle of wine.

"Sir, I appreciate your kindness, but I don't know your name."

The stranger looked into Keira's eyes, drawing her into his enchanted aura.

"Young lady, You have been through so much pain. You have been misunderstood and judged harshly. You are unique with a great destiny. I am here for you."

Keira's eyes began to tear up.

"Let's have a little wine to celebrate our new friendship?" clearing his throat, he continued. "My name is Wanton."

He chanted like he was up to something. As he poured the wine into Keira's glass, she saw a change in his behavior.

"Wanton, I've never had alcohol."

Wanton insisted. "It's all right, Keira; I will make sure you drink responsibly. I have a daughter who is about your age."

Keira grew suspicious of his intent.

She pushed her glass away. "What is that? It's horrible."

Wanton persisted. "Have a little more. You will eventually develop a taste for it."

"I'm not feeling well."

Wanton held Keira's wrist. "I have a place nearby where you can lie down."

He pulled Keira from her chair and left the restaurant, pushing her into his car.

"Let go, said Keira." With a long, pointed fingernail, she sliced his eye.

Wanton became furious. He grasped Keira's hair, tilted her head, and long-jagged fangs stabbed Keira's shoulder to the bone. Keira fainted.

Wanton shoved Keira into the back seat of his car and drove to a motel. He carried her emaciated body into the room and laid her on the bed. Just as Wanton removed her lace panties, Keira began to stir from her fainting spell.

"Stop it; what are you doing." she cried out?" Then Keira blacked out again.

Wanton smirked. "The venom in my saliva and other hidden treasures should knock you out until morning."

Wanton, thirsty for her blood, glided on top of her frail body. A dark shadow suddenly crossed the room, and, Wanton vanished, screaming obscenities. Keira's guardian remained by her side until dawn.

Keira awoke the following day with a splitting headache. She began to cry as she remembered the previous night's incident. She then felt a loving presence around her.

"I do not know who sent you. Show yourself," said Keira.

"It's not time," the spirit whispered.

Keira picked up her bag and was ready to leave the motel when she heard a knock. The door opened, and two police officers came into the room.

"Keira Wolf, Come with us. I'm officer Daniels, and this is my partner, officer Sloan."

Sloan held her by the back of her neck while Daniels cuffed her.

"We have been looking for you."

Keira was angry due to the excessive force they had used on her.

"What do you want with me?"

The motel manager called the station when he saw a young girl carried into the room. Young lady, it is illegal to be on your own at fourteen, especially without financial support. Are you working on the streets?" Officer Sloan asked coldly.

"What do you mean working the streets?"

Sloan, who failed the Communication Training, continued.

"You know, low life's like you get into a little prostitution to survive."

Disgusted by his line of questioning, Keira was just as rude.

"What is your pleasure? Prostitution or a little candy?"

"Are you accusing me of being a dirty cop?"

"If the shoe fits, said Keira."

"My guess is you're a newbie in the sex trade."

"F*** you, dirtbag. Sloan, even if I were a call girl, I would always be too good for you. Worse, you are an embarrassment to the officers who carry out their responsibilities with honor." shouted Keira.

This haughty cop felt a sharp pain across his brow bone, and blood poured from his nose.

"Damn it. I can't stop the bleeding. I feel as though someone kicked me in the face.

I can handle things here. Get yourself to the hospital, said Daniels."

St. Mary's Juvenile Detention accepted Keira as one of their own. She walked through the iron door, where two female guards were waiting for her. Keira removed all her clothing, and the guards searched every cavity on her body. If this wasn't bad enough, the institutional gynecologist crudely gave her a pap test to screen for infectious diseases.

Later that evening, Keira is ordered to take a shower. The house bully entered Keira's shower stall and turned off the water. Regardless of the consequences, this woman gets what she wants.

"I'm Bailey and welcome to my castle. If you stick with me, I will treat you well. If you refuse me, you might not wake up in the morning."

"Lady, you don't scare me. I'm not needy?"

Bailey whispered in Keira's ear. "Honey, you better be needy when I am around."

Keira slowly turned the water back on, thinking about her next move.

"I will stand here all night long until you say yes."

Keira spun around at lightning speed, placed her hand on her throat, and Bailey died before she fell to the ground. Keira ended Bailey's wretched life in self-defense. To avoid being discovered, Keira quickly returned to the dormitory.

The guard entered Keira's room a few minutes later. "You have a visitor."

Keira quickly made her way to the visiting area. A woman in a black robe with bright silver hair sat near the exit door. Keira walked toward the stranger, and she began to tremble.

"Good evening; I hope you are well. Do not worry about the physical reaction you are experiencing; you will soon feel better. I emanate a strong energy field, and often, I forget to keep it under control."

Hannah's beauty and self-confidence were intimidating.

"Who are you, a social worker?" Keira asked.

"My name is Hannah. I have been helping your mother understand your gifts. Now that you are old enough, I will be your guide."

"If you're here to help me figure out who or what I am, thank you but not interested."

"Yes, I saw your cunning moves in the shower stall. If you are not interested, that's your decision."

"How do you know about the shower incident?"

"You are asking too many questions. Our gifts, if you will, are given freely by the universe, Headmaster, and Gaia. We must always use our talents for the right reasons and protection. If we cast spells maliciously, we are cut off and must draw our energies from the dark realm."

"That's too much information for one person to take in. I am sure there are others like me."

"Keira, at the age of six, Headmaster, saw your shattered heart as you sat crying in the church. All those nights you cried yourself to sleep, he collected every teardrop and appointed me to help you evolve into the soul you are meant to be. I can facilitate your journey." Hannah whispered.

"Hannah, my mother, and father do not know what to think of my abilities. They prefer that I live with others like me."

"I am sure they do not believe you are a quirk of nature, just different. Remember, people fear what they cannot see or understand."

Hannah's gold medal, which hung around her neck, caught Keira's attention.

"You're wearing an interesting pendant. It bears no image or engravings."

"It is unadorned for a good reason. Take a closer look, Keira; you will see glimpses of your future." She whispered.

Hannah's medallion drew Keira into another realm. Keira found herself flying over a body of water where humanoid-like creatures are jumping out of the water. She dove in and sank like a rock to the bottom of the sea. Keira saw living beings caught in old fishing nets. She managed to set the living free, then flew out of the water. Keira woke from her trance.

"Hannah, what was that? Those poor creatures said they had lived in darkness for years. I think there are others."

"Keira, you have been in an altered state of consciousness. You were selected to carry the torch of love, life, and healing to the universe," said Hannah."

"Wait, are you saying I had an out-of-body experience? Don't show me anymore; you're creepy."

"You will quickly discover who you are and choose your path. The first step is to accept oneself." Hannah said.

"I'm not so strange," said Keira, looking at her broken fingernails.

"Hannah, soon they are going to come for me."

"You've just sat down, as far as they're concerned." Hannah grinned. "Don't worry about it, Keira; I control the time."

"I'm going to say something that may surprise you. Your paternal father is not your mother's late husband. We are related. Our mothers knew the same man. Your father is from another dimension."

"My father, is what exactly?"

"Our father, Keira, is one of the fallen angels who arrived on Earth thousands of years ago. Andria and Francis drew negative energies, alerting the dark angels to possible recruits. One night after a heated argument with Francis, your mother fell into a deep sleep and was comforted by a dark entity. You inherited his power but not his nature. Had you killed Bailey for anything but self-defense, you would have entered the dark side, never to return. A mortal can return to the light if they venture away. We do not have that privilege because of the unique abilities that we are given at birth. Our gifts are to be used to improve the lives of others," said Hannah.

Keira felt numb and needed time to digest the information. "Hannah, where do I go from here?"

"Follow my instructions, and when it is time, I will come back. Do not change the path of your journey. By the way, Keira, the arresting officer, was disrespectful. However, you should not react to someone's negative behavior; otherwise, you can share their destructive karma." Hannah said.

"I don't know what happened to me. I'm going to keep a check on my temper." Keira smirked.

"That's all for today. Time must be restored." Said Hannah.

Hannah stood up and raised her left hand, and chanted, "Permissum Northmanni vicis recolo. Time resumed."

NINE

CELESTIAL BIRTH

Keira spent four years in the Montreal Correctional Center on serious assault charges. Hannah waited patiently for Keira's release today.

"Finally, I thought you would never get out. Before we go home, I will introduce you to a few friends. They live three blocks up from here," said Hannah.

"Interesting, there is no hello Keira or happy to see you out."

"Keira, I have been a daily visitor. Be thankful your father came to see you once every two weeks. I do not coddle."

Both Keira and Hannah walked briskly toward their destination. Keira felt the hair rise behind her neck.

"What's wrong?" asked Hannah.

"I'm not sure. We are being watched."

"Nothing to worry about for now. Keep walking, and don't look back."

A cold wind picked up as they approached the old antique shop. Hannah walked in, with Keira following close behind. This specialty shop served as a front for the magickal arts. On the left side of the room, simulated crystals hang from the ceiling. On the right, rare diamonds and rubies were collected from the most remote places. Recruits are tested and evaluated at this magickal location and have high vibrational energy to enter Raven's Academy. As Hannah and Keira enter the store, an elderly couple greets them.

"What a lovely surprise, Hannah. I see you've brought a companion."

"Keira, I'd like you to meet Prudence, and her husband, Prodavus.

"It's a pleasure to meet you."

Both prudence and Prodavus had white shoulder-length hair. It's difficult to tell if they are a couple or brother and sister. However, they seemed very friendly. The mist rose from the old wooden floors, and the dust sparkled as the sun shone through large stained-glass windows. Each glass pane is etched with a pentacle. The aroma of rosemary and thyme filled the air. "Finally, I am home," Keira thought as she took a deep breath.

"This place is incredible. I see you appreciate the intricate beauty of crystals."

"You have a discerning eye, Keira," said Prudence.

Hannah led Keira to the center of the room. "What do you see?"

"Hannah, the right side is bright and colorful, but the left side makes me nauseous," said Keira.

"You belong in our world. Your gifts are spot-on for your age. The crystals on the left are imitations and filled with dark energy. The individuals who made them were oppressed people full of anger and fear," said Prudence.

Prudence looked up, and a large stone fell into her hands.

"Take this red ruby and keep it with you. It represents the month of July, your birthstone. This stone represents nobility, passion, protection, and wealth. When worn as an amulet, it alerts the wearer against dangers and protects against psychic attacks. It is a great piece of wisdom. This mighty stone will always find its way back home if it becomes lost. When it glows, it indicates that you are doing the right thing. If the stone turns black, don't go down that path. Keira, something to ponder on. No one can take away your power unless you give it away." Said Prodavus.

Keira had never held such an exquisite gem.

"Are you sure that I should have this precious gift?"

"Keira, this ruby has always been yours. You are a Nephilim, part human, and angel. You lived in another world before you were born on this one, surrounded by precious jewels, said Prodavus.

"Why don't I feel like a spirit being?" Said Keira confused.

"You are still bound to the earth. I will cut off your *Spiritualis Est Praecisus Umbilicus,* and the veil covering your eyes will be removed."

"You're going to cut off my what?" Asked Keira.

Hannah laughed, "your spiritual umbilical cord, silly. It is safe for a Nephilim to do this, not humans."

"Keira, are you brave enough to go through this process? Once your eyes have opened, there will be no turning back." Said Hannah.

"Will it hurt?" Keira winced.

"Painless; however, I must advise you to be accompanied by Hannah for a bit until you get used to your new surroundings. You will see troubling things and do not interfere with the other worlds. Agreed?" Prodavus smiled.

"Yes," said Keira.

"Are you ready? Asked Prodavus. Hannah will become your spiritual mother as a result of your new birth. You must always follow her instructions."

Keira retrieved the ruby from her pocket and saw it was glowing brightly.

"I am ready, and Hannah, I trust you."

Hannah sat Keira in an English armchair used in the nineteenth century by the Duke of Wellington. Prudence placed her fingertips over Keira's eyes and recited a mantra three times. During the chant, Keira saw a raging sea and mirrors shattering while still on the wall. Prudence removed her hands from Keira's eyes, and specks of white dust vanished into the air. The images are dark omens of her future. Keira is filled with energy and feels light-headed. Keira opened her eyes and discovered that everything around her emitted light.

Hannah spoke. "Keira, can you see the energy around you?"

"Hannah, the crystals to your left are engulfed in a dark mist that smells like dirty socks. The rubies and colored diamonds on the right sparkle with the aroma of fresh nutmeg, cinnamon, and a hint of cloves. "What would happen if the jewels were switched?" Asked Keira.

Prudence interjected. "Keira, you are right-handed, so the jewels to the right are perfect. If you were left-handed, then the gems to the left are flawless, as well."

"What if a person is ambidextrous?" Asked Keira.

"Both sides win." Said Hannah.

"Splendid, Keira, you have received your first lesson. It is time for a new session," Prudence said.

Hannah motioned Keira towards the back of the store and opened a large metal door. Keira thought it was one of those walk-in freezers. A majestic sculpture of Michael the Arc Angel stood at the chamber's center. The statue had hair of gold filigree, his body was silver and gold, and he held a sword encrusted with precious gems.

"Magnificent. I detect such a great presence." Whispered Keira.

"Keira, place your right hand on the sword and hold on to my waist with your left hand. You will feel a gush of wind in your face. Now close your eyes." Said Hannah.

Keira opened her eyes and was captivated by the magnificent surroundings.

"Incredible; it is all coming back to me." Said Keira.

Keira and Hannah sat on the patio, watching children running around in the courtyard. Not all the children were perfect. Some were normal-looking children; others had a disability of some sort.

"Keira, every child is waiting for their earthly parents."

"Hannah, why would anyone want to live on earth? It was a mistake to join the human race." Said Keira.

"I don't think it was a mistake. How else can you experience love, compassion, and empathy? How would a person learn courage if they had never experienced fear? Pain is part of life. A person that has never suffered will not understand compassion or empathy. Keira, the earth is a living entity. It can feel, breathe, and is aware of the destruction. It has been scientifically proven that house plants have a psychic connection with their owners. Everything that has life thinks, feels, and reacts as human beings do. Even more incredible is that Professor Ivan Isideovich Gunar, head of Plant Physiology at the Timiryazev Academy, discovered that plants have electrical impulses similar to human nerve impulses. The universe is a living being. I know this may sound crazy to some, but it's scientifically proven. Said Hannah.

"How beautiful," said Keira.

Keira closed her eyes and embraced the serenity that surrounded her at that moment.

"I'm sending you to a place where you'll discover new talents and use them to help others." Said Hannah.

A child with bright green eyes and snow-white hair looked up and smiled lovingly. Keira's heart skipped a beat as she felt this child's love.

"Now it is time to rest. We have a big day tomorrow."

"Hannah, before you go, where is Mathew?"

"Your brother decided on the realm of light. Children can tolerate that specific part of the universe since their hearts have not been dimmed by the evil one. Mathew is living in the presence of our Great Spirit, who is the very essence of love. "Once you've been there, you'll never want to leave."

"Can I visit Mathew?" Asked Keira.

"Keira, we cannot enter such a hallowed place. We will know when the time is right. Now get some shut-eye and be at peace."

Unable to sleep, Keira has decided to explore the library.

Keira walked past the bookshelves, her fingertips skimming over the ancient manuscripts, sensing the magickal essence of each volume.

Hannah and Keira sat on the terrace early in the morning, enjoying breakfast with the children.

"Did you enjoy the library last night? It must be great to reach the top shelf without anyone's help?

"Hannah, the plethora of information in this library is incredible."

"Oh, Keira, I see you are improving your vocabulary. Good for you."

Keira chuckled and said. "I wondered if you would notice."

"At a later date, you can return to the reading room. For now, it is safer if you stay by my side." Said Hannah.

Shortly after breakfast, they returned to earth, where Keira continued her Journey.

TEN

UNINVITED GUEST

Keira sat in Devon's lazy boy, nervously twisting her black tourmaline ring back and forth.

"I have something to tell you, mom. Hannah has found a home where gifted individuals can learn how to develop their abilities. The house can be seen only by people with psychic sensitivity. As new students arrive, rooms are magickally added to the house. I can't wait to leave the city. Mom, imagine waking up to the fresh country air in the morning."

"Marion's chalet is in the English countryside," said Andria."

"This is the most exciting part. If I'm hungry, a waiter in the dining area will bring me whatever I want." Said Keira.

Andria didn't want to hear much more. When are you coming home?"

"I'm not sure. We do have some time off in the spring. our classes begin in a few days."

"So soon?" Andria glanced at her watch. "It is dinner time; we will talk more about this special place later."

Andria pointed and motioned at Devon to get up. "You are peeling the onions."

"Not tonight, love. I have something to do, and it cannot wait." Devon picked up his jacket and left, slamming the doors behind him.

"It is the third time this week. What is your mistress's name?" Andria shouted.

After supper, Keira began to think about a friend that she would be leaving behind.

I will give him a call," Keira thought.

The following day, Keira had just finished washing the dishes when the doorbell rang.

"Keira, how does it feel to be eighteen?" Asked Aiden

"No big deal. It's just another day. Mom bakes a chocolate cake every year, and dad puts a crisp fifty-dollar bill in my shoe."

"Do you think your mother will extend your curfew?"

"I doubt it. Aiden, you know how my mother is? She doesn't want anyone to know her daughter is a tomboy and not as refined as the other girls in church."

"What does your dad think about his daughter's asexual lifestyle?"

My father said, "If you're happy, the hell with the rest of the world."

"Keira, you just turned eighteen, and your parents are still making decisions for you? Others will find that strange. Have you thought about it?"

"Aiden, frankly, I don't care what anyone thinks. I'm living in their house, and they pay the bills. Their house, their rules." Said Keira.

"I don't get it. Your mother is a control freak. How are you supposed to learn about life if she shelters you from the world?"

"Sheltered? I don't think so." She smirked.

"Aiden, there are certain things you don't know about me. It sounds weird, but that's the way it has to be for now."

"We have been best friends for many years, and still, you do not trust me?"

"It is not about trust. If I reveal certain things about myself, our friendship may end. My life is complicated."

"You are speaking in riddles again, and I do not understand," Aiden uttered.

"If you are truly my friend, be patient, and wait until I'm ready to tell you."

Aiden wrapped his arms around Keira and hugged her tightly. Caught up in the moment, Keira passionately kissed Aiden on the mouth for the first time.

Aiden quickly backed away. "I love you as a friend, but I never kissed a girl like that before! Secretly, I wondered what it would be like to kiss you. It was nice, and then again, it felt strange to kiss a woman's mouth."

Keira smiled. "We are best friends, and we don't have boyfriends. I cannot see the harm in it. Aiden, I am sure we are not the only ones that have thought of this. Anyway, we never sexed a boy." Said Keira.

"Speak for yourself; I have dated a few times. Unlike you, I can become intimate." Said Aiden.

Get over yourself. Everyone's concept of normal is different. In society, I'm regarded as a misfit. My last boyfriend described me as frigid and lacking in passion. I couldn't get close to him. Why make excuses for who I am?"

"I am sorry for hurting you; what if my friends believe I prefer the opposite sex? I would never find a partner." Said Aiden

"If you're that worried about what others may think, why do you hang out with me? All I can tell you is to keep your business to yourself. I do not ask my friends if they are heterosexual or gay and how they like it in bed. They may perform certain acts that may not be my cup of tea. It's none of my business, and I don't need to belittle anyone to feel good about myself. When two people love each other, it comes from deep within their hearts and not from sex organs." Said Keira.

Aiden paused before asking Keira a question that may evoke painful memories.

"You have no desire to be intimate with either a man or a woman, Keira. "Did something happen to you that drove you to become this way?"

Keira fell silent. Memories of Matteo flashed through her mind.

"Aiden, I had a terrible experience." Perhaps this is the source of my avoidance of men and women. Let's change the subject."

Aiden and Keira walked through the park in silence, thinking about what was said. They crossed onto an old bridge that led to the neighboring field. Aiden gently pushed Keira against the pillar and kissed her passionately."

"Do not be upset. If you want me to stop, I will."

Aiden gently nibbles on her bottom lip, "tell me what you want."

"I'm sorry, Aiden. I feel nothing. Please stop."

Aiden murmured, his voice quivering. "I love you so much, Keira."

"Perhaps we will help one another heal one day," Keira whispered.

Keira told Aiden later that day that she would be leaving for Raven's House.

Her prolonged absence saddened Aiden, but he realized it was best.

"Keira, I understand why you are leaving," he said, clutching her hand. I'm going to miss you terribly. What happened between us today is a good beginning. We are besties enjoying each other's company."

Keira let out a sigh of relief when she heard Aiden say those words.

"I was afraid that you would be confused. I love you as a brother." Said Keira.

"Whatever I feel for you is nothing more than infatuation. When the novelty wears off, I will be back to normal, said Aiden.

"You will be gone for quite some time. Do not forget to send an email or call as soon as possible." Said Aiden.

Keira packed several suitcases for her flight in the morning. That night, it was chilly, and she decided to wear her flannel nightgown to bed. Keira walked into the bedroom and noticed her frosty breath as she exhaled. An unusually tall being sat in a lounging chair. As Keira entered the room, he stood up.

Startled, Keira shouted. "Who are you?"

"You are stunning," the stranger said. "You have my eyes and my hair. Do you know who I am, Keira? Can you sense it? Perhaps something familiar?"

Keira realized that his power signature was identical to hers.

"Are you my father?" I have been struggling with my identity for a long time."

He walked towards her, ready to take her hand, when Hannah appeared in the room.

"Leave her alone and go." Her voice thundered. "Keira will not become the dark monster you have chosen to be. She is under my protection." Said Hannah.

"No problem; we'll find a way to get rid of you first. My daughter is capable of making her own choices. After all, who do you think you are?" The stranger replied in a hostile tone.

"Are you not curious about your family history, Keira? I've accepted responsibility for my errors and lived with the guilt of failing to communicate with you."

"He's lying, Keira. He hopes to return with you, and the dark queen will use you as a sacrifice. She wants your throne."

Chrysalis knew he had lost this battle. A horrible stench filled the room when he morphed into a winged snake. The odor was so foul that Keira grabbed her rubbish bin and vomited. He flew out the window and faded into the night.

"You are not leaving my side until I get you out of here. Chrysalis has found you, and he will return." Hannah said.

Keira and Hannah dashed downstairs to the living room. Andria was seated in her favorite reading chair, checking her phone for messages

"Hannah, it's nice to see you again. Would you like a cup of tea?"

"Black, please," Hannah replied quickly.

Andria was disturbed by her unexpected visit.

"Is there a reason why you are here so late?"

"Keira had a guest this evening. Chrysalis, her paternal father, wanted to take his daughter home?"

Andria had an inappropriate smile when she heard his name; she collected herself.

"Did he ask for me?"

Her only concern was reuniting with Chrysalis.

"Keira, when I became your mentor, our souls were linked together. When you are in danger, I can see and feel it. Tonight, your fear alerted us when you discovered your father's presence." Said Hannah.

Andria abruptly left the room. She still hadn't returned after an hour.

"Get your luggage, Keira; we are leaving tonight. It is not safe here. Your mother is still under the influence of that demon, and he will use her to get to you."

Hannah looked for Andria to inform her that they were leaving soon. She entered the kitchen and heard screeching noises coming from the basement. Hannah crept down the cellar stairs, and to her horror, Andria was naked in midair. Andria is lying on her back, straight as a board. Her head twisted completely around in an upright position, and she stared into Hannah's eyes. "It is too late for me; this is where I belong. Go away, now!"

Hannah quickly walked back to the living room just as Devon came in from his outing.

"Has my wife gone to bed?" Asked Devon.

"I am not sure how busy she is right now." Said Hannah.

Andria walked into the room as soon as Hannah finished speaking.

"Here I am, just folding laundry."

"Marion has graciously invited us to dinner tomorrow night. We should leave as soon as possible." Said Hannah.

Andria's face darkened because she realized they were leaving.

"Where are you going to find a flight at this hour?" Please wait until the morning."

Hannah grinned. "I own a private jet. It has special features that will get us to our destination quickly. It is now ready and waiting for us."

Keira hugged her parents. "I will write often. At least you won't have to worry about me anymore." Sadly, glancing over at Devon.

"I know you're all grown up, but always remember, if you need anything, I'm here."

"Thanks, Dad, I won't forget."

Andria kissed her daughter on the cheek. "Behave, Keira."

"Mom, what is the matter with you?."

Devon chimed in. "She is in one of her moods again."

A silver Cadillac pulled up in front of the house, and a man in a black three-piece suit opened the back passenger door and helped Keira and Hannah into the vehicle. He then swiftly placed Keira's luggage in the trunk. Re-entering the driver's seat,

Knud turned and said, "you are a beautiful young lady. Yes, indeed!" His eye fixed on her.

"Knud, her name is Keira Wolf. She will become one of our most promising students." Said Hannah.

With a broad smile, Knud politely said. "Please to meet you. I am sensing that you will need extra protection. Am I spot-on, Miss Hannah?"

"That's correct," Hannah said with a scowl. "Her father is the shady Lord Chrysalis."

The smile on Knud's face faded into an expression of concern.

"We need strong protection barriers around the academy."

"Chrysalis? I have heard that name before. Is he an incubus that visits human women in their sleep and has sex with them?" Said Keira.

"He is known as The Grand Master of the incubus and succubus underworld. The succubus has intercourse with men while they are sleeping. According to legend, the incubus or succubus will take advantage of whoever they please, regardless of gender. Your father, Keira, is an angel who refused to take human form. He chose to serve the dark realm, thus the name Chrysalis. Samael, the Dark Queen, has complete control over him. She is more powerful than all previous Dark Lords combined. She is the Mistress of Darkness and the Chief of Dragons." Said Hannah.

Knud interjected. "Anyone who does not obey Samael's every whim suffers a horrible death. Usually, a spirit cannot die. Still, Samael has found a way to torture souls without mercy until the soul returns to pure energy. She rarely uses that method of torture because the power returns to our Headmaster, and we become powerful. Lord Chrysalis cannot physically hurt you. However, he can play with your mind to the point where you will take your own life."

Keira cried out. "What does that make me, a budding succubus?"

"Even if you were solely spirit or part human, you could choose to remain in the light or complete darkness. Never try to use your powers for evil. To venture to the other side can be dangerous. If you are not sure, come to me. I will guide you."

"Hannah, define evil." Asked Keira.

"When the light does not sanction an action, it is defined as evil."

"I don't understand." Said Keira.

"Kill for pleasure or revenge will get you a free trip to the dark side." Said Hannah.

Knud escorted Hannah and Keira onto the jet, and within minutes they were in the air.

ELEVEN

NEW DAWN

Marion's silver hair kinked like an overworked perm due to high humidity. Her dress fluttered wildly, waiting for the plane to land.

"Hannah, how was your flight?" Asked Marion.

"Smooth ride. Knud knows how to handle the plane."

"Hannah, we both know the jet is enchanted." Said Marion.

"Shush, Knud needs to feel useful. He is, after all, over nine hundred years old and has always been a loyal member of the family."

Keira flew into Marion's arms. "I have missed you so much."

"Careful child or we will both be sitting on the ground."

"We were on our way to your house, but Mom decided not to come at the last minute." Said Keira.

"I know all about it. You know how moody Andria can be. I cannot wait to show you around your new home."

"Aunt Marion, when do I start classes?"

"In a few days, just like any other university. Hannah and I are the founders of Raven Academy, and we have many areas of discipline. There are regular academic courses, and on the weekend, you will learn about your sacred birthright."

"I have a heritage?" Asked Keira.

"Keira, your ancestors were witches. One day you'll meet them; for now, let's focus on your studies. You will learn about Wicca as a religion, candle magick, spell work, and other magickal crafts. I could go on and on." Said Marion.

"Interesting, but what about some fun time?" Asked Keira.

"Yes, Keira, you will have time to explore. It's not as bad as it sounds."

"Aunt Marion, are you a demigoddess?"

"I am fully human with advanced supernatural abilities. Your father thinks I am a little off."

"I understand what you are saying," said Keira. "Society fears what it does not understand."

Keira walked through the gate and found herself looking out into the desert.

"Hannah, there is nothing out there but white sand. It is not the England I once knew."

"Keira, this is one of England's hidden gems that only the magickal folk know."

A magnificent sailboat sways across the sand. Two women, dressed casually, quickly lower the ramp.

"Hannah, who are these ladies? Asked Keira.

Hannah laughed. I see a man and a woman in long, streaming white robes. What do you see, Marion?"

"Goodness, I see muscular men in tight jeans who are shirtless."

"This is not your typical dessert. It will focus on your brain's pleasure center and allow you to experience what is most gratifying." Hannah said.

"Is this a test, Aunt Marion? I see two people hard at work."

"Keira, this is where we learn self-control. We must rise above what we see and feel. Mastering this exercise will one day save your life."

"I hope I haven't let you down?" When it comes to my sexuality, I'm different."

"No, you haven't. Keira. Be kind to yourself. "You will experience inner healing and have numerous opportunities to explore your sexuality," said Marion.

"My sexuality is fine as is, undisturbed."

They arrived at a steep path flanked by massive Sequoia trees on both sides. The branches formed an arch to welcome their new visitor.

"They're Huge! Look, every tree has bloomed."

"I give them plenty of love. They are my enchanted children. Every morning, I walk down this driveway with my special brew and chat with them. This Manor was once a house of ill-repute and was known distinctly to the very rich. The young ladies were generously compensated yet severely dealt with if they didn't satisfy their customers. Frequently, affluent people came to visit for occasional escorts and playtime. A beautiful creature impersonated a lady of great importance on a dark hollow's eve. She was interested in a little companionship for the night. Money was no object. The next morning, the kitchen maid found two young women with their throats slashed. Shortly after the murders took place, the brothel closed its doors." Said Marion.

"That's horrible," said Keira.

The pleasure palace once belonged to a wicked sorcerer responsible for the deaths. He was sent to live on an island that matched his crimes. He was never heard from again. The Villa has since gone through several owners. The earlier occupants claimed to have heard horrific cries during the night and feared that evil spirits were haunting the property. Marion and I have been living here for over sixty years, and we get along with everyone, dead or alive." Said Hannah.

"Have you heard those cries?" Asked Keira.

"Yes, they are the voices of long-dead spirits in need of a sympathetic ear. They want you to know that they have the same feelings and thoughts as we do in this realm. There is no need to be disrespectful to spirits or regard them as inferior to ourselves. Once upon a time, all ghosts were human. When we die, we all pass from darkness to light. Unresolved issues will bind us to the mortal realm, where we will remain until our problems are resolved. There are evil entities that also dwell among us." Said Marion.

"What causes an entity to turn evil?" Asked Keira.

"If a person were to take an innocent life or betray The High Counsel of Magick, their alliance would belong to the dark realm. Anything that the High Courts do not sanction is forbidden." Said Hannah.

"Our society mirrors other religions with all its rules and regulations."

"Keira, bite your tongue." Said Marion. "As a magickal society, our vision is to create a safe place where true acceptance of all beings can live in peace without the fear of retribution. The statutes must be respected for this vision to become a realization. There are generations of bigots out to change the world as they see fit. There would be complete chaos without the regulations and penalties to match. Do as thou wilt, but harm none is the only requirement."

"I'm sorry. I had forgotten that people like this existed.

"As you grow older, you will gain more wisdom, and making the right decisions will reap the rewards. Let's get back to my house for the time being."

"Aunt Marion loves to talk. I can't wait to get my day started." Keira pondered.

"The entities in my house are ghosts, as you know. They cannot cross over until they find the answers they need. Their mortal lives have been taken from them by individuals who have no conscience. Perhaps, out of desperation, they took their own lives. Whatever their reasons are for not crossing over to the light, remember they have feelings."

Keira interrupted. "Do you communicate with the dead?"

"Their bodies have died, but their spirits live on. Yes, they will communicate with me occasionally, especially if there are imminent dangers."

"How will I know if the Council sanctions my actions?"

"Keira, if something is not right, you will feel a great weight in the pit of your stomach. I am cautioning you now, do not ignore it."

They entered the villa, and it was so quiet; you could hear the field mice in the walls. Keira felt at home with the eclectic décor. A seven-foot Raven Owl carved of black obsidian stood in the center of the grand vestibule. It proudly sat on a pedestal carved of volcanic rock. Keira followed Marion and Hannah into the living room, and the oil lamps began to flicker.

"You have made a pretty good impression. The house is welcoming you home," Marion said.

"I have been here before; It's a Deja-Vu."

"Keira, you have an old soul and have lived many lives. You have returned to finish your work," said Hannah.

"I do not remember my past lives. What work do I need to finish?"

"You will know when it is time." Said Marion.

"We will take you to your room now. Close your eyes and visualize a black door with a gold infinity symbol." Said Hannah.

In a blink of an eye, Keira is standing in front of her bedroom door.

"Hannah, I can't move my feet."

"Keira, your room is locked."

"How is it locked? The door is ajar!"

"No one will enter your room unless you invite them in. Wave your gemstone over the door."

Keira did as she was told, and a curtain of fog lifted from the entrance.

"Among other things, this ruby is your key."

"Hannah, you keep reminding me that no one can enter my life unless I invite them in."

"Correct, this is the most important lesson you will ever learn. Be careful with who you associate with."

Hannah and Marion are both standing outside the room, waiting to be invited.

"Keira, can we please come in?" Asked Marion.

"Oh, so sorry, please do." Said Keira chuckled.

"Um, I see you will be a hand full." Said Marion.

Keira walked around her room, thinking, "a little color would not hurt. Hannah, why are the walls such a dirty gray?"

"This room will detect your state of mind and change color. No painting necessary."

"Marcus, a third-year apprentice, was the last person to occupy this room. He was an empath who refused to let go of the negative energy surrounding him. The dark side can be seductive. His mentors tried to warn him, but he would not listen. He believed that he was able to handle the situation on his own. He chose to leave school and ignored our guidance." Marion uttered.

"What exactly is an empath?" Asked Keira.

Hannah gave Keira a quick summary to satisfy her curiosity.

"In a nutshell, an empath is acutely aware of how others feel. Empaths frequently blame themselves for attracting negative energy. They can sense another person's pain, how others think, and whether or not someone is telling the truth."

Keira was anxious, and the walls began to darken. "Hannah, I am an empath. Will I have a terrible end?"

"Relax, think about the most wonderful time in your life." Said Marion.

Keira remembered precious moments with Aiden in the park. Soon, she was calm, and her walls were a rainbow color.

Marion smiled. "That was quite a memory. Care to share?"

Keira blushed. "Oh, Aunt Marion, I think you know already."

"Keira, I do not need you to stress over a thing. You will never be alone; we are all connected on this vast plane until you tell us to let go." Said Hannah.

Keira smiled, "That will not happen for a long time."

TWELVE

NEW WISDOM AND POWER

Hannah and Marion reviewed their schedule while eating breakfast. Keira sat quietly, listening to their conversation.

"Keira, are you not hungry this morning?" Hannah asked.

"Where is the kitchen?"

"My dear girl, you do not have the foggiest idea where you are? Look around you."

Keira rose from the table and walked around the dining room. The windows were covered with dark gray curtains, and electrical current vaulted from them as the draperies moved to the slightest breeze. Keira looked up and admired the cathedral ceiling finished in old oak. The most impressive chandelier hung in the center. It featured seven Amethyst crystals encased in gold filigree birdcages, with fire emanating from each precious stone.

Keira beamed. "I feel so different."

"You absorbed all this energy from Amethyst crystals, and now you are ready for today's lesson. Close your eyes and imagine the flames from each stone joining together to form one large flame above your head. Your body and spirit are bathed in light. Said Marion.

Hannah placed her finger on Keira's forehead. "I am stimulating your tertia oculus, the third eye. This is your psychic vision. Once awakened, you can see and communicate with other life forms."

Keira smiles. "That's what I call wireless communication."

Hannah laughed. "It's one way of looking at it."

"Keira, close your eyes and visualize what you would like to eat. A waiter stood by the table with the food items that she saw in her mind, "wonderful," Keira cried out.

"Why would you eat pizza, onion rings, and root beer for breakfast?" Asked Marion.

Keira smiled and brazenly replied, "Because I can."

"Keira, I like that side of you. Take care not to offend your classmates. If you have an inflated sense of your importance, your vibrational energies will be lower. You will have to wait a long time for your powers to return, and there will be a cost." Marion said firmly.

"Like what?" Asked Keira.

Marion gave Keira a look that would scare anyone into conformity.

"I get it, Aunt Marion. I'll have to wait a long time for my powers to return."

Hannah interjected when she saw a frightening expression on Keira's face. "You will receive extensive magickal training for the next five years, and your thoughts will be monitored. Keira, your life has been tough, and your self-esteem is at its lowest. Now that you are discovering who you are, great inner healing will occur. Hold on to what this home offers, and your life will change forever. You will eventually have the confidence to master any task. I must remind you again to stay away from that place of degradation, your father's abode."

"Should I decide to follow him, what price would I pay?" Asked Keira.

"Possibly the shedding of innocent blood. Usually, a family member."

"That's senseless," replied Keira.

Marion redirected the conversation. "Enough of that for now. We have a lovely day ahead of us, so let's get started."

"I am sorry, Marion," Hannah whispered. "I had no idea Keira was so sensitive."

"No worries. It's better to warn Keira now rather than try to bail her out later." Keira was on her way to the bookstore when a sweet fragrance of Jasmine caught her attention. Over by the stock room, Keira spotted Hannah and a boy unpacking boxes.

"Keira, come join us," said Hannah

"Hannah, do you work here?" Keira asked.

"The first few weeks of school are the busiest. Laurence's Business Program requires forty hours of work experience. I am just keeping him company."

Keira couldn't take her eyes away from Laurence. His big blue eyes and shaggy golden blond hair drew her in. Hannah noticed the attraction between them. If Laurence could have kissed Keira at that moment, he would have.

"There is a celebration this evening. Our Headmaster will be initiating our new students to Raven's Academy. I'm not trying to scare you, but one of the guards noticed a dark figure lurking near the entrance gate early this morning."

Laurence slipped his hand around Keira's arm and held on tight.

"Good idea." Said Hannah. "From now on, the buddy system is in place. No matter if it is a bathroom break."

"Hannah, do we get to take our showers together? After all, the buddy system is essential." Laurence said with a sly grin on his face.

"Now, you two, I don't want to know about this," Hannah joked.

"Off you go, Marion is waiting to sign out your books," she said, waving her hands in short, sweeping strokes.

Professor Browning, a magickal historian, bumped into Laurence and Keira as he left the teacher's lounge. Keira felt Browning could see their deepest secrets with a single glance.

"This is why we should not text and walk at the same time." Professor Browning grumbled.

"Professor, we don't have our phones with us." Said Keira.

Professor Browning was far too proud to admit he was oblivious to his surroundings.

"Why else would you run into me? Those wretched phones must have been hidden in your bags."

Keira and Laurence said nothing; as luck would have it, he may be one of their professors.

"Are you enjoying your first day of college? Goodness, I am sensing a little fear. You found out about that character who is lurking outside the gate. I am sure Hannah told you about the buddy system, and keep in mind; that your combined energies are much stronger."

"Sir, are we safe?"

"Yes, Laurence, as long as you stay inside the grounds' secured area.

"Thank you, professor; we feel much better now."

Keira whispered. "One of the students might open the gate and let the intruder in."

"Keira, you are shrewd. True, the enemy can enter through other students. All the more reason to be vigilant. We have a protective shield around each student, rendering malicious entities powerless when entering Raven House."

"Professor, Raven House appears to be a center for homeschooling. We hold our classes in the sitting rooms, library, and patio." Said Keira.

"True, we despise the institution's cold and isolating atmosphere. We could have built a magnificent building. Be as it may, neophytes need extra attention. Without the extra help, they fall by the wayside, never reaching their full potential. Students who come to us are those who have been pushed aside by other magickal schools. Advanced students are assigned the responsibility of mentoring students who have difficulty with magickal tasks. Ravens House offers an undergraduate program that local universities oversee. Our students can graduate from their chosen degree if we follow their curriculum and standards."

Then Professor Browning swiftly walked away, leaving Laurence and Keira with more questions than answers.

"What a strange man!" Laurence commented.

"You gain strength, courage, and confidence by every experience in which you stop to look fear in the face. You can say to yourself; I lived through this horror. I can take the next thing that comes along."
Eleanor Roosevelt

THIRTEEN

DO NOT BE DECEIVED

"Aunt Marion, how did you enter my room without an invitation?" Asked Keira.

"Don't you remember; Hannah and I are linked to your soul until we are not needed?"

"Oh, that's right, I forgot."

Marion draped a fabulous gown over Keira's bed.

"Aunt Marion, the gown is trimmed in real gold. Everyone knows I don't wear dresses."

"Keira, your grandfather, chose this dress for you. There is something else you should know. Your father is the headmaster's son."

Headmaster is my grandfather?"

"Sometimes, I'm drawn to the underworld. What will happen to me?"

Marion took the dress and placed it in front of Keira to see how it fit.

"Only you know whom you shall serve. Ask yourself, Keira. Are you drawn to the dark side, or is your curiosity getting the best of you? Careful, the fine line between good and evil is not discernible." Whispered Marion.

Naturally, Marion made a dramatic exit and vanished into thin air.

The lights went out shortly after Marion left. The temperature dropped, and Keira's lips turned blue as glowing white orbs flew through the air.

"What are you looking for?" Keira said, her cold lips trembling.

A small child's spirit appeared at the foot of the bed, followed by Marion and Hannah.

Keira sighed with relief. "I'm so thankful that you are both here. What is going on?"

"Keira, during the witch trials in 1692, Rosa, who occupied this room with her mother, mysteriously died at the age of six in a boating accident. Her mother was accused of witchcraft and was burned alive a few days later," said Marion.

Rosa returned as an orb, and the lights came on soon after she had gone.

"This is quite the place. I never know what is going to happen next."

"You must turn away if you see dark orbs. They're up to something nefarious. Those wretched beings have no power over you, but they can put you in a bad mood. How else can you learn about their world but in the security of your home? Enough for today. We have a reception to attend. Marion will meet you in front of the reception hall entrance." Said Hannah.

Keira was taken aback when she entered the ballroom. Diamond-cut crystal rose bowls filled with crackling energy serve as table centerpieces. The container's radiance illuminated the room. The walls were covered in climbing vines of purple and white roses. Keira picked a grapefruit-sized purple rose, and at once another flower sprouted in its place. Marion and Keira glided to their table.

"I thought places like this were an illusion created by Hollywood?"

Marion chuckled. "Where do you think they got the idea?"

Hannah and Laurence entered the hall and sat at Keira's table.

"What a handsome dinner jacket, Laurence," said Keira.

"Yes, my son look's good tonight. Said Hannah."

Their meal arrived, along with a glass of sparkling water. Marion sneered at her beverage. "As always, alcohol is not permitted here."

Marion discretely retrieved a small flask from her purse and spiked her water.

Headmaster took on the form of an androgynous being with fiery eyes and ankle-length golden blond hair. He wore a black robe and a thick gold chain around his neck with a bright red ruby. The well-lit urns paled in comparison to his brilliance. The students were taken aback by his beauty and began applauding.

"Good evening. If your curiosity does not get the best of you, I see a bright future for you. Students who use dark magic to control or harm others should fear me. Acolytes accepted into this prestigious training program received a valuable gem. This stone will always find you if it becomes lost or misplaced. Please hold this jewel up to your hearts," said Headmaster.

Keira and Laurence held the stone to their chests. The gem immediately embedded itself into their skin, leaving a glint of color to indicate its presence.

"This stone will no longer be with you if you choose to be my rival. It will disintegrate, leaving you defenseless against the enemy. Those who dabble in the dark arts will feel tenderness as the stone embeds itself. It will heal if you are loyal. Be safe, my children, and have a good evening." Said, Headmaster.

Keira is deep in thought and picking at her food.

"Keira, something seems to be troubling you," said Marion.

"I keep thinking about what I want to do after graduating." There is a lot of pain in the world; perhaps my gifts can help. I want to reach out to people whose lives have been ruined by psychopaths with a twisted sense of power and greed."

"If you feel strongly about helping others, you may be drawn to Law and Security. Let me know what you have decided in the morning so that we can change your syllabus."

"Laurence, Keira, get up on that dance floor before the music is over." Said Marion.

Laurence boldly extended his hand.

"Sure, why not." Said Keira.

They couldn't have been more intimate. Laurence's body was firm as if he were bodybuilding.

Laurence whispered in Keira's ear. "It's time to play."

Laurence's lips lightly caressed Keira's neck. "You smell so good. I hope we can do this again."

Saddened with the public display of affection, Hannah gave Laurencece a stern reprimand.

"Laurence, what has gotten into you? It is a special celebration. Save it for later."

Holding back his laughter, Laurence replied. "Oh, mom, you are so old fashion. It won't happen again. Well, not here, anyway."

Keira and Laurence giggled as they left the building.

"Laurence, you know how to get a woman's attention."

Laurence and Keira saw a horse-drawn carriage parked outside the main gates.

"I wonder who this belongs to?" Asked Keira.

"Who cares. Let's try it out. Oh, wait, I have to go to the men's room. I will be right back."

Keira entered the horse-drawn carriage and was surprised to see Laurence sitting there, holding two glasses of red wine.

"Laurence, you don't usually drink."

"Tonight is a special occasion."

"How did you get here so fast? I didn't see you get into the carriage."

Laurence smiled. "Just another perk, thanks to Mom."

Laurence placed his hand on Keira's knee in an attempt to get beneath her gown. He kissed her passionately. "I need you, Keira. I know you want this, so don't push me away."

Keira whacked his junk. "What is wrong with you?" Keira shouted.

"Give yourself to me. I will always be here for you. The more we get to know each other, the better it becomes."

"Laurence, our relationship must be based on friendship and trust. Being impulsive is not my way. The wine is going to your head."

Riled, Laurence added. "I thought we liked each other?"

"Laurence, I like you, but sex is not necessary at this point in our relationship.

"Keira, loosen up and stop the miss goody two-shoe routine. We are both young adults. It's our time to be free, without the emotional baggage."

"Our lives should be enjoyable and full of new experiences. But we're not ordinary people. We live in two worlds that make our lives difficult. Living in the natural world allows us to take risks. Have you considered the magkical realm in which we live? The dark queen is out to seduce whoever she can. We are hybrids, Lawrence, and we must be careful not to fall into her trap."

Laurence laughed. "Keira, you used the word hybrid as if we were automatons. Hmm, the term is Cambion for half-demon offspring."

Stunned by Laurence's comment, Keira furiously replied. "How dare you call me a demon? My father must have been different when he met my mother, or I would not be going to this school!"

The carriage door opens, and Laurence is standing there.

"Keira, where have you gone, too? The party is in full swing, and the games will start any minute now. Hannah moved Laurence aside and helped Keira out of the carriage. Keira became white as a ghost looking for a place to hide. The person she thought was Laurence had turned into black ash.

Hannah shudders. "Everyone, get inside quickly and sound the alarm."

Laurence ran up to the Raven Owl in the foyer, firmly laid his hand on the lava rock pedestal, and sounded the alarm. Hannah sent everyone into the grand hall. Headmaster rose and hovered above the tables. "We had a failed attempt by the enemy. Be vigilant and always refer to your stone that has been set close to your heart. Do not be deceived by anyone." He hollered.

Headmaster glanced over at Keira and dryly said. "I do not need a horse-drawn carriage." Then, He gradually faded away.

Hannah held Keira's hand as she questioned her about what had happened with the imposter.

"Keira do not be afraid to tell us all about it. I know that you are frightened.

We need to get all the facts to protect ourselves from this deception."

Keira wept from her traumatic experience. Marion put her arm around her.

"Now, start from the beginning and tell us what happened."

"We were standing at the entrance, and Laurence said he had to use the men's room. This handsome cab was at the front gates, so I decided to get in."

Keira hesitated and looked up at Hannah, who gestured to continue.

"I saw Laurence sitting next to me, with two glasses of wine in his hands. We kissed, and he tried to have his way with me. I pushed him away. The next thing I knew,

Laurence opened the carriage door, and the person sitting next to me was a mass of ash and dirt." Said Keira.

Marion took a breath to compose herself. "Keira, the time has come for a more dignified living. You are not a child anymore."

"Aunt Marion, what happened in that stagecoach?"

Hannah interjected. "Keira, that she-devil is getting desperate. Her followers are impersonating family and friends to lead you into a trap."

"I should have known that it was not Laurence; he was nasty and smelt funny. Hannah, did you not sense that I was in danger?"

"Keira, the stone embedded in your heart has weakened our link to you. This ruby is going to have more protection than we can deliver."

Keira had mixed feelings about what had happened. She was embarrassed for being duped and guilt-ridden for placing the academy in danger.

"Didn't the stone warn you about this imposter? Asked Marion.

"I had a feeling of heaviness and stinging around my stone. I ignored the warning signs. At the time, I thought it was my skin that was trying to adapt to the ruby.

"Keira, possession has been going on for a long time. Half of the spirit-like beings were thrown out of the kingdom for disloyalty. Until the great deluge, they remained on earth. A group of people had survived, and dark angels inhabited their bodies. There are several schools of thought about how the Nephilim came to be. Some believe that they are the offspring of fallen angels and human females. Others believe angels merely possessed the bodies of human males and mated with human females. No one knows what happened." Said Hannah.

"Queen Samael rose to power, and the bowels of desolation opened." Marion continued.

"I believe that loathsome presence sitting in the carriage with you possessed an innocent person and manipulated your mind to see what it wanted you to see. In this case, it was Lawrence. The imposter's body incinerated when it was no longer needed. I hope all of our students are present." Said Hannah.

"It has been a long day, and tomorrow is all about relaxation and fun." Said Marion.

Keira excused herself, still troubled by this horrible experience. "I am going up to my room."

FOURTEEN

BROKEN CURSE

Keira woke up out of sorts, and her mood heralds a day of quick thinking. Her first class in magickal ethics had already begun. She hurried down the slick corridor, hoping not to trip. Keira speaks to herself when she is alone.

"What kind of first impression will I leave if I'm late for class? If I keep going at this rate, I'll break my neck. I don't require spells or enchanted herbs. I've visited other worlds, levitated at will, and done serious damage with my thoughts. We are poles opposed. Keira's mind filled with negative thoughts, and guilt overcame her. Keira's racing mind continued without an end in sight. She was soon nearing her class when she heard someone call her name. "It sounds like Aunt Marion."

Keira walked further down the hall and drank from the water fountain.

"Keira, now is the time for a little introspection. Do you remember what we talked about at breakfast?" Marion's voice echoed down the corridor.

"Aunt Marion asked me about my attitude. I recall my father quoting a verse in the Bible when I was a little girl, NLT Proverbs 11:2: Pride leads to disgrace, but with humility comes wisdom."

Finally, Keira arrived at her first class, rushing into the room and stumbling over her own feet. Keira blushed with embarrassment as the other students sized her up, wondering who that bungling girl was.

"There goes any pride I had left," Keira said.

Keira awkwardly picked up her books and sat at a desk.

Professor. Hunter is annoyed with her dramatic entrance. He's a tall man with a thin build, long braided white hair held together with a black ribbon.

"Punctuality is not your thing. You must be Keira Wolf, the only student that has not signed in."

"Yes, sir, I apologize for the interruption. If the floors were not so slippery, I do believe I would have arrived on time."

"Chatty, aren't we miss Wolf? Now open your book to the first page. "As I previously stated, magick ethics will be the most important topic in all of your classes." Keira lowered her gaze to avoid making eye contact with the teacher.

Professor Hunter went on. "Your actions and attitude toward your peers will determine whether you are a good fit for this school. We are fortunate to learn the craft as free people. Whatever the case may be, some believe that our teachings are evil. Some will not accept us, no matter what we say. As a final note, magick must not be used for vengeance or mischief. Using magick from anger will rebound on you, and it always comes at a high price."

A student raised his hand. "Yes, Nicholas."

"Sir, our textbook tells us that dark magick is dangerous."

"Nicholas, dark magick requires payment in return for services. The darker the spell, the higher the price to be paid. If the individual is protected, the curse will rebound onto the person who cast the dark magick, and payment is still required. This fee may ask for a loved one's life. When I speak of dark magick, I am not describing the type of spell itself.

Spells are energies that call upon from the universe, earth, or a deity. The energy is a vehicle on which your intention hitches a ride. It is a person's intent behind the charm that is wicked.

Power is neither light nor dark. Never use your magick to hurt a living thing. Otherwise, you risk crossing over to the dark realm."

Keira lifted her hand. "Sir, what if your life is in danger?"

"Good question; what type of danger are you speaking of?" Asked Professor Hunter.

Keira's voice was barely audible. "Physical harm, Sir."

"We use enchanted gems that embed in the skin. This is the real world, not Hollywood, where actors snap their fingers, and nothing can touch them. You will be taught how to use logic and defensive magick to ward off negative encounters in my class. Have I answered your question to your satisfaction, miss Wolf?"

"Yes, Professor, said Keira.

"The teacher doesn't know what I am talking about," Keira whispered to herself.

"Finally, class, respect for self, and others are necessary. Your homework will be a thousand-word essay, double spaced on self-respect, respect for others, and why it is essential? Class dismissed."

"Keira, may I speak with you?" Professor Hunter uttered.

He pulls up a chair and is seated across from Keira.

"I saw something disturbing while I was answering your question."

"Professor, I am afraid of magick." Keira blurted.

"Why is that, Keira?" He asked.

Nervously, Keira continued. "Self-preservation has had serious consequences for someone who threatened to end my life if I did not comply with her wishes. I experienced a strange sensation in my stomach. At that moment, my fear left me, and I felt the energy coursing through my veins. I touched her forehead, and she fell to the floor. The girl was found dead the following morning. I felt justified in knowing she would not hurt anyone else, followed by regret. Professor, I am afraid to be drawn to the realm of evil. Well, since I was." Keira stopped in mid-sentence; the blood drained from her face, and her body shook as she remembered that horrible night.

Professor Hunter gently wraps his long, warm fingers around Keira's wrist, receiving images of the night the beast could have brutally raped her. Her guardian saved her.

"Keira, something terrible occurred the night you encountered the beast. He bit your shoulder and deposited his seed in your bloodstream. Before we go any further, I must summon our Housemistress. Keira, you do not have to say anymore. I saw what happened." Said Professor Hunter.

Marion walked into the class with urgency. "Professor Hunter, what happened?

"Marion, are you aware of Keira's encounter with the serpent, which I believe was sent by the dark queen?"

"Yes, professor. That night the beast impersonated her friend Laurence."

"No, Marion, I am not speaking of the carriage incident. That serpent sank his teeth into her shoulder and deposited his seed in her body."

"Professor, there must be something we can do?" Said Marion.

Professor Hunter had a worried look on his face.

Keira panicked. "What? Cut it out of me, now," said Keira.

"What I am about to tell you may be hard to understand. You must put those memories out of your mind. Do not entertain hate or bitterness. That monster is going to receive what it deserves. Remember, all negative emotions will block your ability to practice your natural talents. Our gifts are a part of us. Without them, we are incomplete."

"Where is fairness in all this? How can I forgive that queen bitch? All I see myself doing is brutally stabbing her repeatedly." Keira whispered.

"Keira, be careful of what comes out of your mouth. You are calling out to the evil one," said Marion.

"Keira," the professor hesitated, looking for the appropriate words.

"Wanton was trying to possess you. Demons have no morals, so they will go to great lengths to get what they want. Your deliverance from this curse is not going to be pleasant."

"Professor, I imagine Chrysalis is the same way?" Keira asked.

"Your father has chosen his path. He is what we call the lost soul who has not decided to come to terms with who he is. We must choose which side of our allegiance to support or risk becoming perpetual wanderers. If you like the evil in this world, you will remain in the dark when you cross over. Sylvia Browne quoted, "With power comes corruption and ego-gratification." Said Professor Hunter

Marion wrapped her arms around Keira's shoulders. "When I think back to all the horrible experiences you've had, starting with Francis' psychotic behavior, Matteos the pedophile, and now Wanton, Your pain end's here.

"Aunt Marion, who was the person who impersonated Laurence?

"I am sorry to have to say this; it was a demon sent by your father. This dark force took down your defenses by impersonating someone you liked and trusted. Do not blame yourself for that."

Professor Hunter took a bottle of holy oil from a black leather bag.

"Keira, before we begin, you have to repeat these words three times and mean them. If you are not serious, this curse reversal will not work."

Keira closed her eyes and started reciting the spell, struggling with every word coming out of her mouth. She battles the darkness that comes into her mind as she chants.

"I let go of my anger, hatred, and unforgiveness to my creator. I am releasing my enemies to the universe."

"I will anoint you with this sacred oil, and your healing will begin immediately."

Keira braces herself for an unexpected effect and becomes agitated as if a swarm of wasps is trying to split her chest open.

"Professor, I am terrified. What is happening to me?

"Hold on, Keira; this will be over soon."

"Alright, Professor, let's get this over with."

Keira continues to repeat the words she was given as Professor Hunter anointed her forehead, the back of her neck, the palms of her hands, and her feet. Keira's body temperature is rising rapidly, and she is sweating profusely.

"I feel sick to my stomach. I think," then Keira begins to vomit, and a nest of snakelets lay dead in the toxic fluid.

Keira looked up at the professor in horror. "Repulsive."

Professor Hunter is alarmed by what he has seen.

"Keira, this person who tried to take advantage of you will return. You see his mark, and he has claimed you for his own. Fortunately, the curse has broken. Now you can protect yourself."

"What are those things, Professor?"

"Diabolus Draco," the professor answers with contempt. "This is also the name of this demon. His kind will strip you of your identity and destiny. But he must wait until you cross over to his realm of evil. He deposited these creatures inside you that night to expedite your transfer. These things are programmed to take over your mind, and eventually, you will develop a form of dementia.

"What now?" Keira asked.

"Keira, you are safe with our protection and guidance at Raven's House. Wanting to be loved is natural. How you manage your relationships will determine whether you live or die. Do your homework before you jump into anything. Do you understand what I am telling you?"

"Yes, Professor. I am asexual and determined to remain that way." Keira said.

"Good. Now I have to clean that up before the next class comes in."

Professor Hunter detected Keira's thoughts. "Keira, it is just as deadly on the floor as in your stomach."

He poured the remainder of the oil into the liquid. Nothing was left but a few drops of bubbling oil. As expected, the foul substance burst into flames.

"You saved my life." Said Keira.

"You made the right decision to trust me. Keira, you have great gifts. Learn how to control each one correctly. Many types of magick are excellent, but they become idle without proper training. As of this moment, you will have to protect yourself from the evil one and take nothing for granted." Said Professor Hunter.

Pointing to the stone embedded in her chest, Keira asked.

"Aunt Marion, "this stone, will it not protect me?""

"Keira, do not be misled; this precious ruby can only guide you out of the basic snares that help the inexperienced. It will grow in strength as your magickal knowledge expands. The day will come when your stone will become useless."

""Professor, may I ask why you retain the title of Wizard? Hannah said we don't have any labels in our realm."

"That's correct, Keira. We have done away with labels due to the stigma it leaves behind. There are a few hypotheses on the origin of the word wizard. The word wizard goes back to the middle ages, and perhaps it began even earlier in Egypt. Individuals who were skilled in the occult were wise men and women. (witches) There is so much more to it. We have good computers in our libraries. I believe a little research is in order. As for me, I do not mind being called a wizard."

The professor reached over and anointed Keira's frontal lobe with his tears.

"You are never going to be troubled with racing thoughts again."

"Professor, how did you know about my thoughts?" Ask Keira.

"I was healed of a similar condition, and I became sensitive to other people who have mood disorders. It is a part of life. Racing thoughts burn energy. An individual who struggles with depression and anxiety will inadvertently draw strength from others to regenerate."

"Thank you, Professor."

Keira laid her hand on her stone and instantly found herself in her bedroom.

"I like this!" Keira said.

Professor Hunter shook his head, surprised at her advanced abilities.

FIFTEEN

LESSON LEARNED

It was midnight, and Devon was still working on a business proposal for his next meeting. Hannah appeared in his study without warning.

"Hannah, why are you here so late?"

"Devon, I'm concerned about Keira. Chrysalis is determined to persuade her to join him. He could manipulate Andria to gain her trust. When this demon has finished with your wife, he will absorb her chi to strengthen his life-essence.

"What is Keira's significance to the underworld?" Asked Devon.

"To obtain the throne, the dark queen must possess Keara's pure essence."

"Keira's father is the Headmaster's firstborn, and for centuries, His throne has been handed down to the eldest child. Chrysalis, my father, has been disinherited and removed from the family lineage for obvious reasons. As his eldest daughter, I was next in line and presented with the crown. I turned it down. All that responsibility is not for me."

"Hannah, you would have made a beautiful Queen," said Devon.

In jest, Hannah continued. "Are you flirting with me, Devon Wolf?"

"Would it be out of line if I were?" Devon uttered.

"I enjoy the attention, but if you knew who I was, all that interest in me might quickly fade away. Devon, let's not make this visit about us." Said Hannah.

"Yes, you are right, but this conversation will not be forgotten," Devon whispered.

Hannah smiled. "As I was saying before you began to flirt with me, the only hope we have is Keira."

"You were a great sorcerer once, and you can be again," said Hannah.

"A sorcerer?" Devon scoffed. "There was a time; I believed that solid psychic ability was all I needed to perform powerful magick. I have taught alchemy for many years, and a few of my spells worked. My students call me the blundering Professor.

"Devon, excessive pride is going to take you down. Jealousy and anger will negate your powers because others are more powerful. Supernatural gifts are freely given for a specific reason, not for profit but to benefit others.

To manifest great power, you must be connected to the spirit world."

"If only I had known. Why hasn't anyone told me about this?"

"Would you have listened?" Asked Hannah.

"Alright, you made your point."

"Devon, You are not alone. The energy you drew came from the earth and what you could absorb. Skilled practitioners are using other resources in their craft. The universe has an infinite supply of energy. There are different cycles and specific times to draw the power we need. "said Hannah.

"Yes, I should have picked up on it before. I have noticed how practitioners' homes looked run down at a specific time of the year, and at other times their properties are pristine. It appears to be a continuous cycle of decay and regeneration.

"Your understanding of the supernatural is increasing, continue." Said Hannah.

"Come to think about it; during my last year of university, I studied this information for my final exams. It is humbling to know that I am nothing more than a grouping of molecules in this universe that vibrates at a frequency between 62 and 72 Hz when healthy." Said Devon.

"Oh, Devon, you are much more than a molecular structure. Now that you understand the forces around you, I must warn you that abuse of authority will destroy you. It is not for people who lust for power and control. I will introduce you to our Headmaster. He can give or take away power. Some call him the Great Spirit and others Creator." Said Hannah.

She stretched out her hand, and Devon held on tightly. They arrived at their destination and stood in a corridor of quartz crystals. Hannah and Devon stood in front of an oak archway.

"I can't enter the room; my legs won't move."

"Wait until you are invited," said Hannah. "As I said before, no one will enter your life unless you invite them in."

"Come in; I do not bite very hard," said Headmaster.

Devon walked in and was surprised at how homey it all seemed. Everyone sat in oversized chairs.

"Well, I am sure you did not come here just to gawk at me," Headmaster said with a contagious laugh.

"I would have expected to see some great mystical room with angels singing," said Devon."

"Devon, what you see around you is for your benefit. I have created an Earth-like environment.

The headmaster laid his hand on Devon's chest and placed a powerful stone under his skin.

"Devon, do not be afraid; this stone is there to protect you. It is made of Moldavite stone and set with diamonds and a Dragon's tear, which acts as an energy activator.

You are a mighty warrior. Hannah will show you how to harness your powers. Use your new gifts only when you need them. Now leave this place and start your journey."

Hannah took Devon's arm, and within a few seconds, they were standing in his study. Devon was lightheaded and sat quickly in his chair.

"Your life would have ended if you had stayed any longer. The incredible energy that your body has received will cause some discomfort. You will get used to it."

Hannah sat down and placed her finger between Devon's brow and began to transmit the information needed to help him understand his new abilities. Overwhelmed by such a vast amount of data, Devon closed his eyes.

"How am I expected to remember all this?"

With a reassuring tone, Hannah said. "The information will come to you naturally when it's time. Get some rest; your journey will begin soon."

SIXTEEN

R E C K L E S S

Queen Samael's long dark hair and seductive green eyes are hard to resist. Sparsely dressed, the queen sat on her throne, parting her legs to taunt her minions. She has the dignity of an ape.

"Chrysalis, you have failed to convince Keira that life with us is magnificent. I'm still waiting." Samael growled.

The queen's face began to contort, and her skin color became a deathly grey, revealing her natural appearance.

Samael screamed. "Must I do everything myself? I need to absorb her noble essence; only then will I sit on the king's throne, and Keira will be my lover."

"Do you lust for my daughter? Samael, I am your lover, and no one else will take my place." Said Chrysalis.

Samael chuckled. "No one will ever take your place. But you do not have a woman's touch. Get out of my sight, and do not return without her."

Determined to present his daughter Keira as an offering of his love, Chrysalis left for Raven's House with a new plan.

The clatter of the lunch bell echoed through the grounds. James, a first-year student, spotted a young man wearing a Ravens Academy jacket outside the gate.

"Hey," James called out, "what are you doing off the estate. It is dangerous out there. Get back into the yard before you get in trouble," said James.

"I'm sorry, I forgot about that."

"Are you a new student? I'm James."

Standing at a distance, the young man said, "just call me Chrys." "Chrys, what? You must have a last name."

"Never had one," Chrys uttered.

They both stood by the entrance of the house. James entered the academy, expecting Chrys to follow. James looked back, and Chrys was still standing by the door.

"Chrys, just don't stand there; come on already; classes begin in five minutes."

The skin around James's stone began to itch, but he paid no attention to it.

"Chrys smiled with a sigh of relief. "I'll be right there."

Chrys needed an invitation to enter the academy and have full access to the building.

Chrysalis waited until James was out of sight and made his way to the basement. Historically, if anyone ventured into the dungeons without permission, the confrontational specters would cling to the individual, causing great hardship until their dying breath.

Marion's cottage was a brothel, and if the girls did not please their clients, they were left naked in a cold dark dungeon for days. Some died of hypothermia in the middle of winter. The women developed a black hatred in their souls and vowed to destroy anyone who disturbed their peace. However, Chrysalis was the exception. The dungeon spirits remembered the pain he was able to inflict.

Within moments of Chrysalis' arrival, the stone embedded in everyone's chest began to burn, a warning that dark forces had entered their haven. James sat at his desk and was in great pain, making it impossible to pay attention to Professor Quigley's lesson.

"Now observe, close your eyes, and begin to imagine sitting on an eagle's back."

Mrs. Quigley began to levitate several inches off the floor. She turned around to show off her abilities and noticed

James' facial expression of pain. She abruptly dropped to the floor.

"James, my boy, what's wrong? Are you ill?"

"Professor Quigley, my chest is burning."

She opened his shirt and saw a hideous sight. The skin around his stone was inflamed, and black matter began to ooze.

"James, we have to go to the infirmary right away."

Professor Quigley took James' hand, and whoosh, they immediately stood in front of Hannah and Marion. Hannah sat James on a cot, and she began to ask him about his recent activities.

"James, what have you done? We are aware of a dark force entering the school. Did you see or touch anything out of the ordinary?"

"I have done nothing wrong. A boy was standing outside the gate, and I told him that we were not allowed out of the schoolyard. I waved the fellow inside. Then he stood at the entrance door." James paused. "Well, you know what happened next."

"Why haven't you alerted one of your teachers to verify his identity, James? It is simply common sense. Did we not teach you about the enemy's deception? Your negligence may endanger the academy." Marion said

"James, have you seen this person around campus?"

"Miss Hannah, I never saw him before, but the boy did say his name is Chrys."

Marion's jaw dropped. "James, did he have a last name?"

"Chrys said he never was giving one."

"Marion, Chrysalis altered his appearance to fit in as a regular student." Said Hannah.

They left James with the nurse and went looking for Keira. Her room was just a few doors down from the infirmary.

Marion was banging on the door. "It's Aunt Marion and Hannah. Let us in."

Keira is screaming. "Come in, help me."

The door flew open, and Chrysalis stood in mid-air with his arm wrapped around Keira's struggling body.

Hannah instructed Keira to lay her hand over her stone for protection. Hannah and Marion held a crystal wand in their hands and together guided and combined the power against Chrysalis. High energy pulsated from their bodies through the crystal rods, magnifying their power beyond measure.

"Father, let go of Keira," Said Hannah.

Chrysalis released Keira and threw her on the floor.

"What are you doing to me?. Stop, or I will return to pure energy. Hannah, how can you do this? I am your father." Chrysalis shouted.

"You never felt anything for me. I feel even less you." Said Hannah.

"This is the final payment required for choosing to live within the boundaries of the dark arts.

"You sold out your daughter to satisfy your selfish needs." Said Marion.

Gradually, Chrysalis began to fade until nothing was left.

"Keira, your father will never bother you again. But how did he manage to get into your room?" Asked Marion.

Hannah interjected. "They both have identical energy patterns. The protective spell surrounding Keira's room identified his insignia as Keira."

Keira sprained her ankle when she fell from Chrysalis' arms. Aunt Marion teleported her to the medical wing and prepared a healing patch.

"There will be no trace of the sprain the next morning."

"Aunt Marion, is he going to come back for me?"

"No. Your father has returned to a place of tranquility."

"Keira, you will inherit Headmaster's power and take his place as the ruler of this mystical world. It is yours if you want it." Said Hannah.

"Headmaster is still by your side to support you. Keira, this is your destiny. You have always known that you were different. The night we spoke of helping others can now become a reality."

"It is a lot of responsibility. Hannah, I am not sure," Keira paused. "Never mind; we will discuss this later.

"Samael wants to drain your royal essence from your blood. Nothing is going to stop her if she succeeds. The planet will eventually become a wasteland, and all living creatures will die, including the human race."

"Hannah, I understand what you mean by my essence. It is like a greedy beast that steals the innocence of a child and then throws that child into a deep dark sewer when done. A thief in the night has taken away their power."

"It sounds like you are speaking from experience," said Hannah.

Keira's eyes became dark. "Hannah, my life is a work in progress.

Forgiveness, unconditional love, and self-acceptance
are the core ingredients for Inner Peace.
M.G Williams

SEVENTEEN

UNEXPECTED
OUTCOMES

The apprentices stood nervously in front of their drawing tables while Professor Crowder demonstrated the fine art of magickal drawing. Keira sat in her usual seat at the back of the room.

"In your last class, you were taught that words can be a blessing and a curse. Never summon something you cannot undo. Words have great power, so use them wisely. Magickal artwork is not for the faint of heart; it can be lethal, and every brushstroke or medium you use must have intent and a purpose. I will demonstrate," Professor Crowder said. The professor began to draw a simple outline of a bird. He swept his hand over the sketch and said, *"Bird of my creation; open your eyes and fly into the sky."*

A snow owl leaped out of the canvas and flew out the window. Everyone was surprised to see such beauty created with just a few strokes of charcoal.

Soberly, Professor Crowder continued. "Now, I will show you what not to do unless you are in control."

The instructor drew a fire-breathing dragon with the body of the Anaconda snake. He pursed his lips, and plumes of black smoke came out of his mouth and covered the image. With authority, he called out. "Awake, you great beast of the underworld."

The creature slid off the canvas and stood ten feet high on the tip of his tail. The fiend unfolded his large black wings behind his shoulders, and his mouth opened; fire erupted from the back of his throat, just a few inches away from the instructor's head.

Keira felt a steel band tighten around her head, then suddenly, she transformed into a great white blazing lion. She wrapped her gigantic paws around the beast, and it was burnt to a crisp, leaving nothing but black earth and ash. Exhausted, Keira collapsed to the ground and reverted to her human form.

"Well, young lady, you have mastered the ability to transform into a creature of your choosing. Shapeshifting is not for everyone. However, I did have the situation under control." Said Professor Crowder.

"Professor, it just happened," said Keira.

"Not to worry, you will soon learn how to control that gift."

Professor Crowder observed his students rushing out of the classroom and shouted,

"I will see you all next Monday, and please keep out of trouble."

Keira returned to her room, ready for a long nap. Not five minutes had gone by when she heard a loud knock on the wall, "come in," said Keira.

Headmaster appeared in her bedroom, whispering, "Keira, relax, and do not be frightened."

This loving Spirit glided to the center of the room, and particles resembling static electricity whirled into a beautiful love seat.

"Come, sit with me," said Headmaster.

"Before I explain my reason for being here, promise me you will never leave anyone to enter your room unless you know who it is. I could have been some deceiving spirit sent by Samael."

"I had such a bad day; I was not thinking."

"Keira, you did an excellent job today. You saved your teacher and classmates' lives.

. We are getting rid of that cursed fear today," said Headmaster.

"Something happened in class today, and I could not control it." "Keira, start from the beginning. What led to your transformation?"

Keira stood up and began to pace around the room.

"Professor Crowder demonstrated the dos and don'ts of magickal drawing.". His last sketch was a creature from the underworld."

"Continue, Keira; you're safe here with me." Said, Headmaster.

"The creature slithered off the canvas, and I felt a band tighten around my head. A vision of a white lion appeared in my mind, and the energy in my body intensified. I destroyed the beast by fire."

"Congratulations, you have won your first battle. You will face numerous challenges until your firstborn inherits the throne. The white lion represents the enlightenment bearers. Keira, your gifts will gradually surface at the right time. Come here and stand in front of me."

Keira is baffled about her firstborn.

"Headmaster, I was not planning on having children. When I think of night feedings and dirty diapers, no thank you."

"No need to think about children right now."

Keira gave Headmaster a curious look.

"Keira, fear, and courage go hand in hand. Having courage involves having enough confidence to face a situation that is intimidating or that can end your life. A healthy measure of fear can save your life, and too much will cripple you. Fear quickly creeps into a person's soul because it is the most effective form of domination. Your parents, religious organizations, militant groups, and society use this type of coercion to hold you in line with their wishes. "I will heal you from this curse," said Headmaster.

Headmaster placed his hand on Keira's stone, and she felt a slight tug. He removed half of her gem and replaced it with a black diamond. Keira's back straightened, and her eyes shone like the sun.

"I feel so different," said Keira.

"I will be with you through all your battles. One day, you won't need precious stones for protection. Think of these jewels as your training wheels. Your fears have gone, and you will become increasingly clever as you mature in your craft."

"Do I have to wear all those fancy dresses when I take over your throne? Too girly for my taste; I prefer my look."

"Keira, do whatever you want."

"Let's begin your healing process. Keira, close your eyes and relax. Imagine that you are entering a temple of white light. Keira, what do you see?

"Headmaster, I see a dense forest teeming with wild animals. I'm walking down a diamond trail to a mother of pearl Pavillion. I see a little girl waiting. She begins to cry as I hold her in my arms. I whispered, "no more tears, sweetheart; no one will ever come between us again." We are one."

"Come out of the sanctuary, through the veil. Now watch the temple fade away. That room no longer exists," said, Headmaster.

"Headmaster, I'm not sure how to describe it; I have a strong sense of belonging. I've spent my entire life carrying shame and guilt that didn't belong to me. Friends and family would invite me to a social gathering, and I would retreat to my dark little corner. I was on the verge of suicide due to severe bouts of depression. I would rather sleep my life away than interacting with other people. I've made bad decisions because I saw myself as worthless, but it's all gone now."

"Keira, those terrible memories will soon fade with continuous healing."

A new chapter in Keira's life has begun.

Keira's feet rose from the floor, and she began to soar and twirl, appreciating this wonderful gift of healing.

"I hope you do not mind if I use my levitation gift. The heaviness that iI have been carrying all these years is finally gone. It feels so good."

"Go ahead; nothing is stopping you."

"I must leave soon. Keira, if you are in danger, the black diamond will pulse quickly. Remember, I am always with you, and behave as though your gifts do not exist; other students may feel left out."

"Do not worry; I would never intentionally hurt anyone."

Keira stared out the window. The garden began to emit colors and patterns she had never seen before. She turned around to speak with Headmaster, but he had left.

Later that evening, an odor of burning rubber suddenly ended her contemplative mood. Keira sat on the edge of the bed, scanned the room, and saw nothing smoldering. She walked down the hallway, and the pungent smell became more robust. Keira covered her nose and mouth with her shirt sleeve and followed the scent to its source. A young woman wearing a black sports bra and matching bikini underwear is stirring a horrible brew simmering in an old cauldron.

With English elocution, the young woman stood up and invited Keira to her room.

"Come on, get in here, hon. I am Erin; what can I do for you?"

Keira walked warily into Erin's room. Many herbs are scattered over the floor, and ancient Greek artifacts and other statues of old gods. There was an altar in the corner of the room with a brass sword, candles, figurines, incense, a chalice, and a pentacle.

Erin saw that Keira could not tolerate the smell of this particular brew.

"Here you go, place this ointment under your nose, just a little something I whipped up. This ointment will reduce the unpleasant smell," said Erin.

Erin and Keira both sat on the floor in front of the cauldron. Erin folds her legs into a lotus pose. Keira peeked into the pot and saw a mixture that looked like chunky brown slime.

Keira quickly backed away. "What is that stuff. I think I am going to be sick!"

Erin giggled. "Do not get your knickers in a bunch. It is just about done. Aren't you the girl who turned into a beautiful white lion in Professor Crowder's class on Friday? You are one of the warriors. There are only five people selected for this mission. We all have different gifts. If one leave's the group, the remaining wizards and witches will receive a portion of their mantel," said Erin.

"How do you know all this?" Keira asked.

"Marion offered me this assignment, and I accepted it. It's part of our training. With a bit of detective work, it is only a matter of time before we discover the identity of the other team members.

"What are your gifts, Erin?" Asked Keira.

"I have a few gifts that everyone receives at birth. I am an empath, and I can fly. I can teleport to another part of the building or anywhere. Watch this; I have been practicing for the last three weeks."

Erin picked up a tree branch and held it over her head.

"Keira, this is my ceremonial staff. This branch does not have any power. Erin mounted the wooden staff like she would a horse and began to hover all over the room. Keira, you could ride anything you like. You have the power, not the object you choose to ride on. You could use your bathtub if you wanted to." Erin uttered.

Keira smiled. "Broom riding started with hallucinogenic plants. The past witches would either eat or lace their broomsticks with a powerful drug. Men and women were so stoned; that they thought they were flying through the air. We do not need brooms; we use the power of teleportation."

"Seriously, where is your sense of adventure. I like feeling witchy and weird," said Erin.

"Erin, becoming a witch is who you are and not a fashion statement. "What other gifts do you have?" Keira asked

Erin transformed into a winged Draco Leonis, part dragon, part lion. Keira had never seen such a massive creature and backed away.

"Erin, you can do some serious damage." Said Keira.

Returning to her original appearance, Erin spoke with great pride.

"Yes, brilliant. When I first began to change into other creatures, I was exhausted and needed power naps."

Erin's concoction came to a hard boil, letting out a belching sound, and the smell had become intolerable. Keira is determined to find out what this stuff is all about.

"What is that noxious smell?" Asked Keira.

"Hey, what's up with all the questions? I hope we are on the same side?"

"No reason, just curious, that's all." Said Keira.

"Fine, if you must know, this is a twenty-five-hour lust serum."

"Erin, I have heard of love serums but a lust potion.?"

"Who is the poison intended for?" Asked Keira.

Erin is becoming annoyed with Keira's inquisitive nature.

"Listen, miss Wolf; this is not a poison. Just an elixir to improve the odds."

"I have been dating this wizard for two months, and he is interested in other women. If I were to give him a love potion, his affections for me would last until the effects wear off. The lust tonic would make him desire me. By the time it wears off, I hope he will only fall in love with me." Said Erin.

"And If he doesn't fall in love with you, what then?" Keira asked.

"My recipe book is overflowing with powerful spells. I am sure I can concoct something a little more potent.

"Erin, his sexuality is being manipulated. If you are not around, someone else or a thing will come along and give him what he wants. You are treading on thin ice. Speak with Hannah and find out what she believes. Please leave it alone and let it happen naturally."

Erin ignored Keira's sound counsel and redirected their conversation.

"I am sensing that you do not care for bell ends?"

"I am not attracted to either sex. I can have romantic relationships. However, sex is rarely on my brain."

"You are asexual? You do not know what your missing, girl. Said Erin.

Fanny girls find this potion unpleasant. It is a calling card to a man's hunting prowess."

Keira scrunched her nose and murmured. "With that stuff, I am sure he will smell you calling for miles."

Erin smiled and nodded approvingly.

"Keira checked her watch. "Dinner is in thirty minutes. You're welcome to sit with my aunts and me," said Keira.

Erin smiled, "will do. See you later."

EIGHTEEN

COOKING WITH A BANG

"Hannah, I asked Erin to join us for dinner this evening," said Keira.

"If she does not arrive soon, she will be eating alone."

"Erin must have changed her mind. The elixir of lust brewing in her room may need more cooking time."

"Keira, what are you talking about?" Asked Marion.

"Erin is brewing a lust potion. The young man that Erin has been dating lost interest in their relationship."

"Did you say lust potion?" Asked Hannah.

"Are you sure?" Marion uttered.

"I reminded Erin of the consequences of working with the dark arts."

An explosion was heard at the main entrance, and smoke fluttered down the stairs from the women's floor.

They heard a woman coughing. Cautiously, Hannah climbs the stairs. By the time she had reached the second floor, the smoke had dispersed.

"It sounds like Erin," whispered Marion.

Keira ran to Erin's room. "What happened here?"

"Come in. It's just a little bang." Said Erin.

Erin stood up slowly, her face covered in thick brown soot. "I'm going to be fine. I feel like a daft cow."

"You're not stupid, but you have a lot to learn." Said Hannah.

"I added a pinch of dragon's blood and cinnamon to the mixture to give it a little oomph. Instead, I got a boom." Erin is still coughing.

"Let's wipe that sticky soot off your face," said Hannah. "Erin, it sounds like this young man has sent you mixed messages. Do you believe a lust potion would have made a difference in your relationship? Sit down with him and ask him where you stand in his life. Whatever you hear, accept it. Most of all, love and respect yourself so that you can choose someone deserving of your friendship. Self-respect is the only power you need, and it is key to attracting the right person into your life. This rule applies to people from all walks of life." Said Hannah smiling.

Marion smirked. "How did you get so wise, woman?"

"I've made that same mistake several times until I discovered that self-respect will take you much further than being needy. There is nothing sexier than a woman who knows where she's going. Remember, girls, respect is not a fad, but a way of being."

Marion and Hannah left the girls to clean up the mess. Spending time together has allowed them to get to know each other. They both had the same question in their minds. Would they either step up to the plate to fight or run if their lives were in danger?

The evening had gone well. Erin and Keira reminisced about their childhood, magick, and love. Erin looked deeply into Keira's eyes and saw a faint image of a white lion engulfed in fire with crystal blue eyes.

"Keira, you have the great lion spirit, Leo spiritus, and boundless courage and strength coursing through your veins. You must have quite a few beauties after you. As for me, I am too straight to be attracted to women. I love the feel of my man's muscular body against mine and other things."

In a reassuring tone, Keira continued. "Erin, I do not want to talk about my sexuality."

"Maybe your kind secretly wants it all the time," said Erin.

Erin's ignorance puts off Keira. People who indulge in bigotry have created an atmosphere of hostility. Many individuals let on that love is love no matter your sexual preference. The truth is if your orientation is not heterosexual, your presence is tolerated only. "My kind? Whether I am gay, straight, asexual, or the color of the rainbow, it is nobody's business what sexual orientation I prefer. I am a human being, and no, I do not walk around wanting honey all day." Said Keira.

"Wow, you do have a flash temper. It will control you if you do not bring it under control." Said Erin.

One of our significant gifts is telepathy. "Do you honestly believe I wanted to have sex with you? Could you not read me? I knew that you were heterosexual." Said Keira.

"Yes, I know. No more lectures, please!" Said Erin.

"Sorry, I became agitated. I am not normally so sensitive. Erin, if we harbor strong negative emotions or flirt with the dark side, our special abilities will suffer." Keira murmured.

Keira knew something was different about Erin. She dismissed it as her imagination.

"So much has happened since my arrival. I am beginning to see things that are not there." Keira thought.

"I have been so preoccupied with this guy; I have been studying the dark arts, hoping to find a simple spell that would encourage him to give me a second chance." Said Erin.

"Erin, this young man is not right for you. He has bad energy, and you need to stop seeing him. Your research in the dark arts will teach you how to protect yourself. Then again, if you intend to use this magick to control his sexual desires, it is crossing the line. Did you not feel your stone warning you?"

"Yes," Erin shouted. "Stop hounding me. I knew this horrible infatuation was going to catch up with me. Our commitment to the cause must come first."

"Erin, you are not alone anymore. If you need to talk things out, I will always be here for you."

Erin's telepathy came rushing back. "I am going to be okay, Keira."

Erin paused and looked at Keira, wondering why she was not attracted to her.

"Am I not good enough for you?"

Keira grinned. "You're back to normal, all right. Even if I were interested, I would not kiss you with all that slime on your face.

"Well, come to think of it, the slime could be fun." Said Erin.

"Umm, I do not think so; besides, it is getting late." Said Keira.

Keira found a clean spot on Erin's forehead and gave her a peck.

"Sweet dreams Erin."

Erin thought if Keira were a man, she would be the perfect mate. Halfway down the hall, Keira yelled out, "Do not go there, Erin!"

NINETEEN

BEST FRIEND OR LOVER?

Andria had fallen into a deep depression and had considered suicide. She stopped bathing, ate little, and cried a lot. She was hospitalized for a few weeks until she could function independently. Devon suspected it was because Chrysalis had not visited for a while.

Devon informed Keira he was one of the five members of her team. Delighted, Keira began to fire one question after another, not waiting for answers.

"Calm down, Keira; let me say something.

"One night, Hannah appeared in my den, scaring the hell out of me. We talked, and the next thing I know, I am having a meeting with Headmaster. He was well aware of my years of witchcraft experience. When your mom and I were first married, living with a sorcerer frightened her. So, I ended my practice. Keira, your mother, has become distant, and she will only speak if she's spoken too. At this point in our lives, I believe that if I return to my craft, your mother won't care one way or the other, said Devon.

"Dad, I miss her. Mom will not go anywhere with me. Keira whispered.

"Don't lose hope. I have a meeting this morning, but we'll continue this conversation later tonight."

"What's for dinner?" Devon asked to lighten up her mood.

"We are going out for dinner," she replied playfully.

Keira's cell phone rang.

"Aiden, I was thinking about you this morning. I have been trying to reach you all summer."

"I'm on my way over, Keira. I have a lot to tell you."

"Hurry, I can't wait to give you one of my bear hugs again."

Keira splashed a little perfume around her neck, hoping Aiden would notice.

Aiden arrived with a sad look of uncertainty and sat at the dining room table, sipping on his tea.

There was an awkward silence between them.

"Aiden, you seem a bit nervous this morning. I picked up on it while we were chatting on the phone.

Aiden was confident that he would not lose his nerve if he spoke quickly.

"It's been ten months since we last spoke. Shortly after we parted, I fell in love with this fantastic person, Chip. Last Friday, we visited his parents. Keira, I am so happy, Chip is wealthy, and we fell in love instantly. I will spend the rest of my life with him."

"Aiden, I didn't think you were that shallow. You fell in love with Chip for his money?"

Keira studied Aiden's face, not wanting to believe the words that came out of his mouth. The enthusiasm in his voice does not match the sadness in his eyes.

Aiden's sadness is knowing this news would break his best friend's heart.

Keira wanted to believe that he was in love with her. Evidently, Aiden's gender preference in a mate was male.

"Aiden, are you sure? It hurts to think that you are with someone else. Have you told him about how we feel about each other?"

"Keira, it's our secret." Aiden snapped.

"Keira closed her eyes and whispered, "Aiden, I should have known better than to feel something for you. I will never forget our time together."

"Our friendship does not have to end. When we marry, you can sit with us at our table." Said Aiden.

"How can you ask me to be at your wedding? Do you know how I feel about you, or did you forget what we had last summer? Aiden, you never cared about me."

"Don't say that, Keira. You know how much I love you.

"My family would not understand why I should give up a life of comfort for a fling with you?"

Hurt by Aiden's arrogance, Keira reacted. She abruptly stood up and threw her tea in his face.

"A fling? Oh, that's right, god forbid you should be seen with a person like me. Think of the reprisals we'd have to face."

Keira paused for a moment to regain her composure. "Love yourself for who you are, and others will too."

"Enough; I don't want to hear another of your self-esteem lectures," Aiden uttered.

Keira could not understand how insensitive Aiden had become.

"Sorry, I don't feel the same way about you. We experienced a deep affection between best friends and not lovers." Said Aiden.

Aiden got up and walked to the door with tears streaming down his cheeks.

"Keira, Chip is waiting for me. Are you alright?"

"I will be fine; kiss me; it will give us closure, said Keira."

"Our feelings are too intense. It is better that I go now," said Aiden.

"You are your best friend." Said Keira.

Without hesitation, they kissed passionately. Aiden wanted more, but Keira stopped him.

"Not like this, Aiden. If I were to make love to you, it would be difficult for us to remain friends. You decide what is suitable for you."

"Keira, I don't have your courage. I care about what people think of me."

"That is the difference between us; I do not care about what anyone thinks; it is my life, not theirs. I am leaving for school tomorrow morning. If I don't hear from you, it is over." Said Keira.

"Right now, I am so confused. I need some time to think about it," said Aiden.

Keira watched him drive away in his new Porsche, wondering if she'd ever see him again.

There was no sign of Aiden as Keira's ride pulled up in front of the house. Keira sat on the patio swing, watching Knud load her luggage into the car's trunk.

"Miss Keira, are you waiting for someone?" Asked Knud.

"Aiden has decided to stay home today. Chip must be an exceptional person."

"Cheer up, Miss Keira. You are still young."

TWENTY

MASQUERADE BALL

Soon after Hannah and Keira boarded the jet, Knud landed behind the villa in Marion's old apple orchard. The oak trees near the entrance gate displayed their autumn leaves, and the heavy clouds laden with rain did not improve Keira's mood. The weather was freezing for this time of year. The boys shuddered in their thin tweed jackets, and the girls hurried into the building with their short skirts. Keira was ready to eat her lunch when she saw Erin and Laurence enter the dining room. She stood up and gestured the couple to the table.

"Keira, I am so happy to see you again. How was your vacation?" Asked Laurence.

"Bittersweet. I had a few family issues to deal with over the summer."

"There's something different about Erin." Keira thought.

Erin and Laurence smiled at each other, remembering their good times while traveling together.

"Erin and I went backpacking this summer and made new friends." Said Laurence.

"Wonderful, tell me more," said Keira.

"Something weird happened. We left for Ireland and decided not to use magick while on our trip." Said Erin.

"Oh, that is roughing it," said Keira.

Laurence continued. "We visited many little shops and discovered one we both loved. It was called Snacks & Cauldrons. Once inside this charming restaurant, a sign pointed to another door that led to an enchanted room. Excited about our find, we both ate quickly and shopped for new altar covers. Time was going by so fast. This mystical place had herbs, crystals, candles, cauldrons of all sizes, etc."

Erin interjected. "Laurence picked up a clay brooch. It had an image of a dragon with the body of an Anaconda."

"How odd," said Keira.

"Examining the object, I remembered the creature in professor Crowder's class. Keira, I am sure you remember transforming into a flaming white lion and killing it."

"I will take it from here," said Laurence. "Without warning, the pin leaped from my hands and latched on to my bottom lip. I began to scream from the pain when an older crone appeared out of nowhere and abruptly pushed Erin aside.

"You stupid child, what have you done to yourself?"

"The woman held a small vile in one hand, and blood from my lip began to run into the ampoule.

"This is plenty for my spell," said the witch, and then she vanished along with the trinket."

"Blood magick is dangerous with un-practiced hands but deadly with the experienced wizards or witches with evil intent. You will need a counter curse. Laurence, please tell Hannah about your experience. You did not meet this sorceress by accident," said Keira.

"Keira, you are making a big deal out of this situation," said Erin.

"Erin, the old crone, took Laurence's blood. Ask yourself why? It has to be a blood spell," Keira said curtly.

"Why would a stranger do something like a blood spell to a boy she has never met before?" Said Erin.

"If you can both stop arguing, I'll continue with my story. We left the shop without purchasing anything. I needed to forget about the ordeal, so we used magick and quickly returned home."

Keira pleaded, "Laurence, promise me you'll tell Hannah about your experience."

"I will, Keira. The school is throwing a costume party tonight to welcome back the students. I am going to talk to my mom about my trip tonight." Said Laurence.

Erin's fingers caressed Laurence's hand while Keira gave a few highlights about her summer holiday.

"I can see that you and Laurence are now an item. Are you giving new love a chance?" Asked Keira.

"I'm always open to new adventures," said Erin.

"What happened to the person you were dating?"

"You were right; he was not a good fit."

"That's good; you were obsessed with him."

"There you go again, so damn nosy. I already told you; I dumped my boyfriend, so drop it."

Laurence is stunned by Erin's behavior. "Relax, Keira is concerned about your wellbeing."

Laurence felt awful for not giving Keira a head's up about his relationship with Erin.

"We were just buddies, Keira. Our relationship was at a standstill."

Keira raised her hand to stop Laurence from explaining anymore.

"I am fine with you and Erin. No hard feelings."

Keira liked Laurence, and she enjoyed the time they had together. Laurence was fun-loving and generous in every way. Unfortunately, there was no chemistry between them. On the other hand, Aiden was all Keira wanted in a partner. Aiden appeared cheerful and outgoing, but he suffered from severe depression. His mother struggled to support her six children. Aiden, the eldest, assumed the role of an adult, caring for his siblings, and had little time for himself.

Unfortunately, his mother engaged in fraudulent activities to put food on the table.

Eager to experience a new year of mysteries, students from all over the world returned to Raven Academy. Keira was happy to be back for another year, and it was the distraction she needed to get over Aiden. The laughter was heard all over the house. Walking out of the dining room, Keira heard Marion calling her name. Marion stood by the library door with an enormous black owl.

"Osric, I would like to introduce a team member." Said Marion.

"Aunt Marion, is this beautiful bird part of my team?"

Osric quickly became a human male with black shoulder-length hair and golden-bleu eyes. His tanned complexion was flawless. Keira backed away, stunned by Osric's transformation. Again, he morphed into the most beautiful woman Keira had ever seen. Her long, chestnut hair brought out her bright green eyes. She wore tight blue jeans and a black satin shirt.

Osric smiled at Keira's trance-like state."

"Was it pleasant for you, Keira? "Based on your expression and heightened pleasure, I have exceeded your expectations," said Osric.

"I don't know why you behave this way; I am not impressed." Said Keira.

Keira, I did not reveal my natural powers of persuasion. Can you imagine what would have happened if I had? Your level of excitement would have been overwhelming. That is just one of my many skills. Please don't tell me lies, Keira. I can scan your mind." Osric beamed.

"Osric, you need help. You have a sick mind. I forgot to place a hedge of protection around my mind and heart this morning. I promise you it will not happen again." Said Keira.

Keira was self-conscious when she reacted to Osric's transformation.

Osric changed his appearance once more and became an eagle owl.

"Osric, you are a changeling," whispered Keira.

Marion interjected. "A baby boy was born to a beautiful sorceress. Her name was Rebecca. One night, her son stopped breathing and living in the middle of a vast forest; nobody was around to help her. Rebecca's magick was not strong enough to bring him back. She summoned the Lord of Hades and requested the return of her child. The child would not take a breath until a human witch found him. In exchange for the child, she gave up her life.

We had a wind storm one night, and most of the village was destroyed. My house was the only building that withstood this vicious gale. I walk around the property to check on my trees the following day. From a distance, I saw a tree with several of its branches touching the gravel road, supporting a small round object. I picked up the sphere, and the tree branches rose from the ground." Said Marion.

"What was it?" Asked Keira.

Headmaster placed a protective shield and a blessing around him to prevent this dark lord from coming back to claim him for his own. "It was my precious Osric. I became his mother. Keira, he is your first cousin." Said Marion.

"Father never told me about a cousin!" Keira muttered.

"He never found out. After all, it happened about two hundred years ago."

"Aunt Marion, did you say two hundred years? Can you live forever?" Asked Keira.

"I have had several past lives. When my time is up, I cross over to your grandfather's realm, and he renews my life cycle. I will live until our work is finished. I chose to remain here for another term." Said Marion.

"My father has no idea that you have lived for so long. That is awesome." Keira murmured.

"One day soon, he will know everything going on." Said Marion.

Osric began to communicate his thoughts telepathically. "It's not for Marion's ears."

Keira rolled her eyes as he shared his thoughts.

"I know we are not blood cousins. Yes, Osric, I know you can become the woman or man of my dreams. Hey, you horn dog!" Keira said.

Keira started walking away, "Just a moment; I have something for you," Marion said.

Marion placed a gold medallion around her neck. "It can link our souls to one another. Keira, this pendant will never leave you. If you need our help, please call out."

"You make it sound like my life is in danger."

"You know who we are up against, and the time is coming when we must fight."

Keira's heart dropped at losing the people she loved to that miserable dark witch.

"Yes, it's still on my mind. One day soon, it will be over. Until then, I have to get ready for the party; I have not decided what to wear."

Marion smiled. "I am sure you will figure it out, Keira."

Keira hurried back to her room and began searching through the closet. Keira opted for a gold shimmering wrap-around evening gown with a revealing V-shaped neckline. Keira added a little gel to her hair and lightly tasseled the curls to frame her face. She was just about ready to leave when her stone began to vibrate. Keira saw only the ruby was in motion. "Osric will be up to his old tricks again, she thought." Her stone shone brightly, a positive sign that she was right. Most of her friends were married, and she was standing at the bar without a partner. Osric did his best to keep her company for most of the night but decided to pursue a nice little empath.

Keira spotted a handsome young man with curly black hair sitting alone at the end of the bar. She walked over and sat down beside him.

"You are the only man wearing an oversized football jersey and a bathing suit. I would not mind a little company?" Said Keira.

"Of course. It is better than being alone. What are you supposed to be?" The stranger asked.

Keira smirked. "Just being myself."

"I'm Cristian, and you are?"

"Please to meet you. I'm Keira."

"Yes, I know you're in my alchemy class," Cristian uttered.

"Cristian, would you like to dance?"

"Hmm, you have been reading my mind," Cristian said.

"Sorry for that," said Keira.

Keira held Cristian's warm, fraSloan body against her.

"You smell so good."

"I am not wearing cologne. Would you like to discover other sweet spots?" Cristian whispered.

Keira loved Cristian's' adventurous charm.

"Do you have more than one?"

"Seek, and you may be surprised."

Keira slips her arm around his waist. "Cristian, follow me."

Keira led Cristian out into the garden behind a large shed.

"Is this place suitable? No one comes here, and we are hidden from the public. We have a bench to lay on."

"Keira, have you been here before?" Asked Cristian.

"Yes, I did. I sit on this bench and read my favorite book in the afternoon.

"What are you reading?" Asked Christian.

"The Avenging Black Rose by MG. Williams."

Christian is in the process of removing his clothes.

"Christian, do not bother taking your clothes off. We are trying something new.

"I want you, Cristian, but not physically," Keira said softly

I am one of those people who does not like to be touched. Intimacy sometimes frightens me. I would like to have a sexual supernatural connection with you.

Psychic lovemaking. How did you know that I am asexual? Asked Christian.

Pleased, Keira replied, "that makes two of us."

Keira held the back of Cristian's head, gently tugging on her hair, and kissed him passionately. Keira admired his bronze body and gently leaned him back on the bench.

"Close your eyes, Christain, and relax every muscle in your body. I will remain by your side. Can you feel my energy floating above your body?"

"Keira, are you rubbing my stomach?

"Not at all, Christian. I am not touching you. Now relax."

Their energies merged, and the connection was complete. Their psychic bond was more profound than the ocean. Keira and Christain remained in enchanted pleasure for two hours without physical contact.

"Cristian, you are not like anyone I have ever been with. There is something about you. Why do I feel such a connection?" Keira asked.

Keira checked her stone, and there were no alerts.

"This man is safe, thought Keira."

"Remember, Keira; there is no such thing as coincidences."

Keira and Cristian walked back to the hall, and there was an awkward silence.

"I enjoyed our time together. Can I see you again?" Asked Cristian.

Keira held Cristian's hand. "Tonight, it was magickal, but I can't make any promises. Making love to you the way we did, was therapeutic." Said Keira.

"What do you mean by therapeutic?" Asked Cristian.

"A special friend of mine recently broke my heart, and I have been trying to get over him. Tonight, he didn't come into my mind, and to be honest, I can only be a friend right now." Keira said mindfully.

"I understand. Maybe we can get together soon."

"I'd like that." Said Keira.

"I'm exhausted; my bed is calling me," said Cristian."

"Goodnight, Cristian. Sleep well." Keira smiled.

"I will be thinking about you, Keira," Cristian murmured.

Keira entered the hall and sat at the bar with Osric. "Where is your pretty little empath?"

"I tucked her into bed. Something tells me you had a little entertainment tonight. Would you like more?" Said Osric, moving closer, ready to kiss the back of Keira's neck.

"Back off, Osric," said Keira.

The doors opened, and the bright lights from the main entrance illuminated the hall. A man entered wearing a black tuxedo and headed toward the bar. Keira was unable to recognize this mysterious man. He wore a mask that hid most of his face, exposing his luscious lips. Now facing each other, the stranger seductively nipped at Keira's bottom lip and said, "Has it been so long that you have forgotten about me? "Keira rose from her chair, trying to identify his familiar voice. The young man takes off his mask and holds Keira in a warm embrace.

"Is that the fragrance of another man? Now that I am here, you are mine, and I forgive you," said Aiden.

Keira was shocked to see him. "Aiden, there is nothing to forgive. I'm single, or do you not remember? The last time we spoke, you were getting married to Chip. I waited the next morning, but you did not show up."

A surprise guest walks onto the stage. The audience went mad with excitement.

"Oh my gosh, Keira, this man is bigger than life," Aiden said. Listen, he is singing our favorite song, "Unforgettable," Aiden softly whispered.

"Let's dance and tell me what you have been up to. Remember how we enjoyed listening to this music while sitting around the campfire?

"You can't just step back into my life and carry on where we left off," Keira said.

"I screwed up, Keira. We all make mistakes; please give our relationship one more try. If we are not compatible, we still have our friendship. I won't have to go through life wondering if we were meant to be."

"It has been a while since I have heard from you, and I have dated since we split up. If you can accept that, I am willing to try again." Said Keira.

They held each other with such tenderness swaying to the music.

"Aiden, I hope we do not regret this.move."

Keira pulled Aiden back and looked into his eyes, searching for reassurance.

"Aiden, are you sure about us?"

"Keira, nothing in this life is a sure thing or forever. Chip was a nice girl and very rich. I do love her."

"Are you sure it is not her money you are after?" Asked Keira.

"So, are you saying you are in love with Chip and me?"

"Keira, I am not sure what I'm feeling. I do love you; please do not send me home."

Keira led Aiden out into the rose garden.

"Marion came by and made an offer that I could not refuse. Keira, I had already decided to end it with Chip while driving home that day. Marion placed her hand on my forehead, and I felt strange. It was like I was given new eyes. Even my skin has become more sensitive."

Keira was delighted at the thought of making love to Aiden as she did with Christian, especially in his new state of awareness. Aiden's eyes were filled with tears, and his voice softened,

"It was so difficult not to see you again. My feelings for you grew stronger as we spent more time together. I never expected to fall in love with you in this way. I had no idea what was going on with me until now." Said Aiden.

"I thought it was over between us, Aiden," Keira said.

Keira had her doubts about their relationship. What she experienced with Christian would not happen with Aiden. Aiden is the physical type, and he will eventually tire of Keira's asexual behavior and attitude.

"Keira, I understand what you have been trying to tell me. In three months, I will be twenty-one, and my parents will not have a say about whom to marry or anything else for that matter. I want us to last forever," said Aiden."

Aiden spoke with a sincere heart, but Keira knew their relationship would be brief.

"Aiden, you must be exhausted. Let's go up to my room. Hold on to my waist and close your eyes."

Promptly, Aiden found himself standing in Keira's room. "How did you do that?"

"I'm going to take a shower, and then we will talk later," said Keira.

After a long steamy shower, Keira walked into the bedroom, and Aiden was fast asleep.

TWENTY-ONE

FIGHT OR FLIGHT

Heavy snow fell on Christmas morning, and Raven House was cooler than usual. Keira showered while Aiden waited in the dining room. Sliding into a pair of jeans, she felt the hair behind her neck stand up. She scanned the room and saw nothing. Although her Talisman was not activated, Keira chose to approach her day with caution. She noticed a dark figure outside the main gates when she looked out the window.

Keira entered the cafeteria, and she was pleased to see the Christmas tree bright and lively. The apprentices artfully crafted the decorations, enchanted candle flames swayed with the music, and luminous frost covered the tree. The chipmunks hopped from one branch to the other, and the barnyard owls, with their eyes half-closed, were ready to fall asleep.

"Keira, sit down and have your breakfast. It takes you forever in the morning. I am starving." Aiden shouted.

Put off by his behavior, Keira shrugged her shoulders and said, "you could have started without me."

"What's the point? I'm still waiting for you to finish."

Hannah interrupted the argument. "What are we going to do for Christmas?"

"I don't know about you, but I have gift shopping to do for every member of my family," said Aiden.

"Aiden, we do not need money around here. Give me your list, and I will make it happen," said Keira.

"Keira, Christmas is all about going from store to store and spending a lot of money."

"How much do you need?" Asked Keira.

"Let's start with two thousand dollars. I will text you if I need more."

"Aiden, are you sure it will take that much?" Asked Keira.

"I know you can afford it, love."

Keira saw a side of Aiden that left a bad taste in her mouth.

"I would like to volunteer in the soup kitchen, serve a few meals at lunchtime, and then hand out gifts to the children. After all, the holidays are about sharing and supporting each other." Said Keira.

"That sounds great, but I will be busy this year. You go and have fun." Said Aiden.

Keira was beginning to see that Aiden had become a selfish gold digger.

Hannah walked into the room, looking agitated.

"Keira, I'll meet you in the conference room in ten minutes; please don't be late." Hannah vanished into the swirling white fog.

Hannah had requested that the team gather in the meeting room. Keira hushed.

"Why are we all here?"

"We had an unexpected visitor. Osric noticed an intruder lurking around the estate last night."

"What are we up against?" Keira Hissed.

Osric cupped his hands, and a ball of energy formed. The sphere of power rose, and they found themselves in a holographic setting. They saw a man's failed attempt to open the gates. He was not successful because of the protection spell surrounding the property.

Keira felt a chill creeping up her spine. That monster was the one who tried to take advantage of her. Keira became enraged and dashed toward him, realizing he wasn't real.

"Where is the beast now?" Keira screamed.

"We are hoping that he is not too close. We need some time to finalize our plan of attack. "Said, Erin.

Devon sighed. "The Dark Queen is running out of options and will try to strip you of your birthright. This demon hopes to reach you before the dark queen decides to make her move."

"I am getting fed up with this power struggle." Said Keira.

Devon continued. "Unless the evil mistress holds the master's children hostage, our kingdom will not be defeated. Your energy is the most powerful force we have against the enemy. We've seen the Dark Lord, who will take over your throne if the evil queen fails."

A great sadness came over Keira's face. Her father is a disgrace. Chrysalis' refusal to accept Keira as his daughter rather than a human sacrifice broke her heart.

"I can't believe my father is part of this horror."

"Chrysalis' was seduced by Samael, queen of the underworld, and became her lover. If you are half-human, there is redemption. Still, a spirit being must be reduced to its primary energy and re-created by Spirit, our Headmaster. Keira, be alert for all sorts of trickery and stay away from physical contact." Said Devon.

Osric interjected. "You don't know who she can impersonate.

"I suppose that includes Aiden; he will not like this," Keira whispered.

Keira returned to her room to meet Aiden for lunch.

"Did your meeting last very long?"

"Aiden, we will have an extended break from our classes. Please go home until it is safe to come back. Something big is coming, and you could get hurt if you stay, said Keira.

"It sounds rather serious."

"Aiden, there is too much at stake. My chances of rescuing you are slim if the evil one kidnaps you. Early in the morning, Hannah will pick you up."

"We can at least spend the night together. After all, we won't be seeing each other for quite some time."

"Not tonight, Aiden. I'm doing this to protect you."

"Protection! Well, there goes Christmas." Said Aiden irritated.

"The money has been deposited into your bank account, Aiden."

Aiden's anger quickly subsided. "Thanks, Keira. The holidays will be a lot easier now."

The following morning Aiden was teleported home to his mother.

"Hannah, thanks for taking me home safely. What if Keira end's up dead, and the last words I said were in anger."

Hannah spoke firmly. "Keira loves you. I don't know why she feels that way about you? Your only concern was money for the holidays. It is much safer at home with your mother. Dangerous forces are wandering around the academy. Hopefully, it will end in a few days. If the enemy abducts you, it will weaken our defenses. Keira and I will come back for you. Promise me you will do as I say." Hannah insisted.

"Yes, I promise," Aiden whispered.

TWENTY-TWO

THE BATTLE BEGINS

"Keira, are you ready? It's Saturday; we don't have to worry about anyone at the academy." Said Hannah.

The clock struck midnight, and still, nothing happened. Keira fell asleep in her chair; Devon soon followed suit.

At 3:33 am, hysterical laughter echoed through the house, and the stench of burning flesh filled the room. The walls shook violently, and they began to crumble. Headmaster hovered to the center of the room and shouted, "Stop," and everything was still.

"It has been a long time, big brother. What are they calling you, Jacob, headmaster, grandad, or Spirit? How have you been? Oh, I can answer that, very comfortable, I presume, in your fancy kingdom." Then the laughter began again, and the stench followed.

"Samael, when will you accept that this kingdom will never be yours?"

"Your sister?" Keira uttered.

I banished Samael for intentionally inflicting pain and suffering on the most defenseless creatures. It was one of her favorite pastimes. She has come for your untainted power to keep her universal throne. Otherwise, she will lose it to Lord Diabolus." Said, Headmaster.

"How can I stop this wicked witch?" Asked Keira.

"Together, we will defeat her." He said.

"Samael, Wasn't Diabolus a former flame of yours? You woke one morning to discover he was gone. I heard he brought along a few of your little sprites." said Headmaster.

"Oh, shut up. I will have your kingdom one day soon." Said Samael.

Samael projected erotic images into Keira's mind.

"Girl, I can offer you endless pleasures and make you feel things that you have never experienced."

Headmaster laid his hand on Keira's head, and the images faded.

"Brother, do not be so cranky." The dark queen said lustfully.

"Could we not have a little privacy?"

Desire filled Samuel's eyes as he stared at Keira.

"I see something oozing from her mouth. I feel so dirty." Said Keira.

Smoke filled the room as Diabolus, aka Wanton, made his grand entrance.

"Samael, my love, I see you've discovered what is mine. "It's good to see you again, Keira," Wanton said, his snake tail slamming on the floor. "Professor Hunter ruined our plans, but we no longer have to worry about him. This evening, the Minotaur feasted lavishly. As for you, Samael, give up your throne; we both know I will win this game."

Samael Smirked. "You're so sure of yourself. My powers will crush you."

Diabolus took off his cloak and tossed it across the floor. He was furious.

"Samael, you idiot, you are nothing to me. You're just a female ghoul, inferior to all-male demons. We have intelligence and the ability to destroy at will."

"Everyone, stand back. Wanton is not going to get away unscathed. Those words are acid on Samael's back," said Headmaster.

Samael morphed into Echidna, a half-woman, half-snake hybrid with a twist. She is a fire-breathing serpent with massive wings. Diabolus transformed into a feathered dragon; a brush of his feathers will kill you. Samael and Diabolus flew toward each other and began a vicious fight. Headmaster had hoped that it would happen. If one were to die, there would be only one demon remaining.

Diabolus had Samael by the throat, and his serrated teeth were ripping her apart. Blood spewed like a waterfall from her neck. She managed to get out of his death grip, and a jet stream of fire came out of her mouth, setting his feathered body on fire. Diabolus began screaming with pain and fell to the floor, rolling to extinguish the fire eating away at him. Although weakened by severe injuries, Diabolus was not ready to give up. He stretched out his seared wings and shot massive fireballs from the back of his throat. Samael then ejected sulfuric acid into his face, burning his eyes right out of their sockets. She wrapped her tail around his neck and squeezed until she heard the crushing sound of his bones and his last breath. Diabolus fell to the ground and disintegrated into ashes. A black shadow emerged from the ruins and vanished into the ceiling.

"Keira, he is dead. Don't be afraid of him anymore. I did this for you."

Osric shouted. "Liar! You did it for yourself. Don't believe her, Keira."

"Osric is right. Samael need's your essence to rule her cursed kingdom." Said Devon.

Keira noticed dark shadows surrounding the evil queen.

"Queen Samael, I am not interested in joining your ranks." Keira bellowed.

"I'll take you by force if I have to. By the way, have you told her who you are, Spirit?"

"There's no need for blackmail; they all know who I am."

Samael extended her hands, and a force drew Keira forward.

"Stop," Headmaster commanded.

Headmaster reached into his pocket and pulled out an iron box.

"Where did you get that?" Samael screeched, "I destroyed that prison when you kicked me out."

"No, Samael. What you destroyed was my prison."

Headmaster placed the small opened chest in Keira's hands.

Keira fell into a deep trance and began to speak an ancient language. She ordered Samael's life force to enter the coffer. Samael began to scream, and she fell to the floor. A great fire consumed her body until nothing remained. Samael's soul quickly settled in the enchanted prison.

Headmaster wrapped his hands around the small chest, and it disappeared.

"Keira, the danger is over. For now, their offspring will soon find a way to claim the throne, and we will have to stand and fight again soon."

"Offspring?" Keira murmured.

Samael and Diabolus have a son, and before long, he will be old enough to take his parent's place. Until then, we wait. Said Headmaster.

TWENTY-THREE

T H R E E ' S
C O M P A N Y

Keira drove up a private road to a stone building covered in thick English ivy.

"Aiden, give me your honest opinion. Well, do you like it?"

"This isn't a house; it's a haunted castle."

They stood in front of an arched entrance, embellished with a Green Man door knocker. Aiden lifted the handle and let it go quickly.

"Keira, that thing is heavy!"

"Not a day goes by that you do not have something to complain about," said Keira.

The door opened, and a voice summoned the couple to come in. As soon as Keira and Aiden walked in, the door slammed shut, sending a loud echo throughout the house.

"You are finally here. Do you like it?" Devon said proudly.

"Dad, this place is stunning," said Keira.

"Despite the older medieval style, new architecture, such as skylights and solar panels, were installed to harness the energy from the sun. The vaulted ceiling makes it appear much larger than it is."

"The house is finally finished, in time for the first snowfall." Keira paused. "I'm impressed. The house is grander than I expected, with all the fancy trimming and a crystal chandelier in the dining room.

"Your grandfather's final touches." Said Devon.

Keira laughed. "Of course, I'm not surprised."

Aiden was not impressed. "Keira, don't you think this is a little much? The dining room is large enough for a family of twenty. Thank goodness for the fireplace, or I would freeze to death."

"Aiden, it is not that big. You haven't included the living room in this space." Said Keira.

"What's up with all the odd lamps hanging on the walls?"

Devon explained. "Aiden, the architecture is a replica of a sixteenth-century castle in Ireland. Because of its size, I have decided that regular electricity is too expensive. We use solar energy for heating, hot water, and power, but there is no internet. We do not have a modem, which means no Wifi."

"That's just great! I might as well grab a tent and live in the forest."

Aiden glanced at his phone. "I have no signal at all. Keira, you can't be serious?"

"We do have a land phone." Said Devon.

"How am I going to text my friends on the land phone? I have to be out in this miserable weather to use my cell."

Keira braced herself for another argument. "Aiden, stop acting like a child. We talked about this a few weeks ago. This place is my home, and it has enchanted protection. Our home will become Raven House soon.

"Marion's villa is an excellent place for Raven's. Why the change of location?" Asked Aiden.

"Marion's Villa will be for novices, while my father's estate will welcome the advanced students.

Aiden took a walk around the house, depressed at the prospect of living without the warmth of his new love.

"I'm going to freeze to death this winter," said Aiden.

Keira took Aiden aside to speak privately. "You've been irritable since we got up this morning. Are you having second thoughts about us?"

Aiden walked away, shrugging his shoulders. Devon saw tension building up between them.

"Come and sit down by the fire; dinner will be ready soon." Said Hannah.

"Aiden, Tell Keira what's going on. We both know that this is not what you want out of life."

"How do you know what I'm thinking, Hannah?"

"It doesn't matter, be honest. Keira already knows how you feel. Chip is waiting. Let's see how dinner is coming along, Devon. You two, cuddle up next to this warm fire."

Aiden took Keira's hand in his and gathered his courage.

"A lot has happened while we've been apart."

"Aiden, I Skyped every night before bed."

"I've changed," Aiden admitted.

Keira leaned back in her chair and sighed. "I see what's coming."

"I value our friendship, but not as lovers, Keira. I didn't understand why I was so upset when I told you about finding someone else the last time we spoke at your parents' house. I was perplexed until Chip and I began seeing each other again."

"I knew something was going on. The chemistry between us is gone." Said Keira.

"I never meant to hurt you. A loveless relationship is not enough. I feel as though something is missing. You once said that we must always be true to ourselves; otherwise, we are living a lie. Chip is willing to forgive me for leaving him. We will set our wedding date when I get home."

"I believed you when you said our love was forever. How can you be so cruel? I was mistaken in thinking that something wonderful would come from this relationship," said Keira with a heavy heart.

"Dinner is ready," said Devon.

Keira wiped her tears away and pretended that everything was fine. Waiters in dark blue tuxedos served a delectable roast beef dinner with all the trimmings. Hannah placed a black candle and a silver goblet filled with a special brew in front of Aiden.

"Drink from this cup and put out the candle. "Your memories of Keira and Raven House will be a dream when you wake up tomorrow morning.

"And how about Chip?"

"Have you told him of what is going on here?" Asked Hannah.

"There were a few instances when I mentioned the magickal work that was going on in our classrooms."

"I expected as much," said Hannah."

Aiden finished his meal and said his farewells.

"When Chip enters your presence, the enchantment from this candle will cover him."

"Our friendship will last forever, and I wish you happiness for the rest of your life," said Keira.

Aiden drank from the goblet and blew out the candle. He quickly fell into a deep sleep.

After their breakup, Keira called it a night. The solar wall lighting on both sides of the corridor allowed Keira to see where she was going. The door hinges squealed as she slowly opened the door and walked into her bedroom. The warmth of the fireplace made it feel like home. Keira sat on her bed and heard voices coming from outside. The floors moaned beneath her bare feet as she crept up to the window to investigate. Except for the enchanted protection surrounding Keira's new house, no ghostly guardian stands at the door to protect her from unwanted guests. Vigilance is now a priority at all times.

In complete darkness, a blue orb floated among the pine trees. Keira assumed the entity was a friendly specter because her talisman did not respond to it. She climbed into bed and slept comfortably, content with her reasoning.

TWENTY-FOUR

SOMETHING IS COMING

The freezing rain lashes the windowpane. It is a miserable way to start the day. Keira had a hearty serving of cream of wheat with plenty of butter and maple syrup for breakfast.

"Ah, comfort food, help us get through this dreary day," Marion said.

"Hannah, I heard footsteps outside my window last night, and I saw a lovely blue orb floating around the yard."

Osric chuckled. "I thought you would scare you; then you would jump into my arms."

"Osric, stop that!" Marion snapped.

"Mom, I was joking." Osric scowled.

Devon interrupted. What is the matter with you this morning, Sis?"

"I tossed and turned all night. Something dreadful is coming."

"Like what?" Asked Osric.

"Be ready for anything." Said Marion.

Hannah dipped a soup spoon into the hot cauldron and began to scoop out a magickal concoction.

"Carefully sip your drink, then watch as visions unfold."

"What is this brew?" Asked Keira.

"It transforms into whatever beverage you desire. Tea is my preferred beverage.

"What have you got, Keira?"

"My usual hot chocolate."

Hannah was the first to sample her potion. "I see deception, evil intent, and power."

Keira sipped her hot chocolate and saw two people dressed in black robes cutting into her wrist. She watched as her blood trickled into an ancient book of secrets.

Abruptly, Keira placed her cup down and stood up. "No!" Keira cried out.

Marion grabbed Keira's cup and handed it to Hannah to examine.

A voice echoed through the house.

"I have been watching over this universe for a long time, and my rule will never end. Soon, I will give you my kingdom. If you return one of my offspring to energy, I will provide them with a new beginning. They will fade into obscurity if they choose to remain evil.

"I have been elusive for millions of years until I realized that my children needed to hear from me. You have seen the destruction of two wicked powers ready to destroy us all. Other Great Spirits appear in a golden mist and give me the teachings. They are mighty beings that cannot be created or destroyed."

A great sadness came over Headmaster's face. "There are labyrinths on the island of Creetus where the Minotaurs live. Their horns are like knives, and their food is human flesh. I sent a dark sorcerer to the island. He gave the Minotaur the ability to become undetectable at will in exchange for his life. The sorcerer was true to his word, but these monstrous giants still decided to feast on him."

"What is a Minotaur?" Asked Keira.

"Keira, they have the head and tail of a bull and the body of a man. And thanks to the sorcerer, the ability to vanish at will. I fear they may have other abilities that we may not know about."

Keira cringed at the thought of coming face to face with that creature.

"Well, I believe my stay will be brief. I see a headstone. Said Devon.

"Do you see markings?" Asked Marion.

"I see the letter A."

Hannah interjected. "It is a warning. Devon, this is not your tombstone."

"No one will enter the library until the timing is right. We will secure the evil one's gateway. If it is closed or destroyed, Keira and Osric will have to stay on the island for another two hundred years. We'll all gather again in an hour for final preparations," said Hannah,

"Keira, you are half spirit and half-human. The more power you receive, the less human you become. Said Marion.

"What if I need a human body?"

"Keira, it would be simple for you to create a body to occupy with all of your power, said Headmaster.

"If these light entities are so powerful, why don't they destroy this evil and be done with it," Hannah wondered.

"That is an excellent question," said Devon.

"The moon and the earth are celestial bodies, but they are not alike. Each has its laws, energy levels, and barriers. If I visit another realm, I must follow its rules and regulations. Not all magick will work on Earth. Some forces will interfere with the levels of energy required to produce the charm."

Marion interjected. "I did not realize that we had to work in concert with all physical laws."

"If our battles were to occur in the spirit world, there would be very little to stop us. Sadly, our enemy has chosen the physical plane to give himself time to change his fighting strategy when needed. Society, in general, believes magick is about producing anything out of thin air. This type of thinking is for young children who cannot understand the laws of physics at any level. Keira, next year, you will learn how to work with different forms of energy and understand why this is another form of life. It may not be the answer you are looking for, but even the light beings must work within the framework of the universe."

"Headmaster, only a daughter or a son can become heir to your throne." Said Marion.

"You are all my children from different worlds. Keira's father is a celestial being, and her mother is human. So, I have chosen Keira to continue my reign."

"Is this why Devon and I carry a piece of your stone?" Asked Keira.

"Yes, at that moment, you both had an instant connection to my power. If you decide that you are not happy with this arrangement, my stone will disappear."

Osric admired Keira's courage. "Keira, do you know how special you are? You have a new beginning and a chance to leave your mark in this world."

"I'm not sure about leaving a legacy, but I understand how important it is to succeed. If I fail, it is the end of our lives as we know it."

Osric pulled Keira away from her chair, "Look at me; you will not fail. We are family, and together we will end this war."

Osric lovingly held Keira in his arms, and a deep bond formed between them that would last forever. Keira returned to her room and rested. She became agitated and cold, wishing she had a cup of steaming hot cocoa to warm her bones. It materialized on her nightstand.

"Here's a first! This usually happens in the dining room."

Her troubled mind was soothed as she slowly savored each mouthful of this hot, rich chocolate. Keira slept after stretching and releasing the tension in her body. "True love breathes life into the soul." M.G. Williams.

TWENTY-FIVE

STRATEGY OF WAR

Keira walks through the forest, and a thick fog obscures her vision. Tree branches softly brush against her face, and she hears a wolf howling. Keira's feet are wet with dew rising from the ground, and her delicate feet hurt from the continuous wounding of sharp pine needles. Keira is lost and becomes anxious as she tries to find her way out. The sun has finally risen, and its warm breath has cleared the mist. She looked down, and mysteriously, leather boots donned her battered feet. Keira hears a voice calling her, and the sound echoes in all directions.

"Who are you?" She cries out.

"Don't be afraid. I will not hurt you! I have no form, and I am not a spirit." The voice roared.

"What are you then?" Keira whispered.

A powerful stream of air coiled around Keira's body and lifted her off the ground.

Keira panicked and screamed. "Stop it!"

The intriguing life form let her go.

"Keira, I am the air you breathe. The ground beneath your feet is alive. We hear you when you invoke the four elements in your rituals: earth, air, fire, and water. We live!"

"I knew you were a life form, but I did not realize you were an intelligent entity," Keira said.

"Keira, you have been given the highest level of authority; with Spirit by your side, no one would dare come against you.

The planet has been suffering for years. Industrial emissions and their inventions have created an environment where we can mutate into toxic substances that destroy all life. Now that Lady Samael is gone, her son will continue what she has begun. Abadon will consume all the energy around him and become more powerful." Said the wind.

Keira heard a loud noise and woke up from her dream.

Osric is pounding on the door. "Keira, are you in there. We're waiting for you."

Rubbing the sleep from her eyes, Keira clumsily followed Osric to the library. They walked toward the old bookcase, and the room suddenly became cold. Keira reached out to take a book off the shelf.

"Stop. Before we explore this porthole, we need a protective shield. If the evil entity attacks us, we have to be ready." Marion cried out.

Marion used sea salt to create a protective perimeter around the meeting table. With each breath they drew, a marvelous light grew brighter. It was a protective field that no entity could breach. Marion gestured for everyone to sit down just as a hefty tome fell from the shelf.

"What is that?" Asked Devon.

Hannah opened the circle and picked up the old book. "I will handle it from here!"

She carefully placed the book in the center of the table, and the old vellum pages began to flip back and forth.

"These are ancient writings that can change the history of humankind."

Devon interjected. "Hannah, is that what I think it is?"

"Yes, the Anunnaki ancestral writings."

Devon sat back in his chair; "this mystery has finally come together.

"The world would be thrown into chaos if it fell into the wrong hands. Fortunately, the sacred teachings were hidden deep in the catacombs of Rome." Said Hannah.

"How did it end up in our library?"

"Devon, let's focus on the matter at hand?" Hannah replied.

Devon began to see a side of Hannah that moved him.

Keira began coughing up blood, saliva running down her chin, her face turning red, and her eyes bulging. Devon tried to get her off the chair, but something held her down. Without warning, he was thrown across the room.

"Help us, Headmaster. We can't see the enemy!" Hannah cried out.

Headmaster hovered above Keira and clapped his hands. The sound of thunder filled the house, and the beast materialized. An Anaconda serpent wrapped itself around Keira's body, slowly crushing her.

"Keira is mine. You should have closed the circle, Hannah."

Devon pursed his lips, and his breath turned into a substance similar to liquid nitrogen, completely freezing the beast's body. The serpent's brittle body crumbled to the floor with one swift blow, releasing its grip on Keira. A black haze lifted from the shattered pieces and disappeared. Osric lifted Keira's limp body off the chair and held her lovingly in his arms. Gradually she returned to her old self again.

Devon is furious. "Headmaster, your power could have killed the beast in an instant. Why didn't you do something?"

Devon, you are all in training. How else are you going to learn to use your gifts? I would have intervened if something had gone wrong."

"What happened to me?"

As soon as Devon explained everything that had happened, Keira was angry.

"Where did that thing come from?"

Hannah admitted her error. "It is my fault. When I picked up the book, I forgot to close the circle. I am so sorry, Keira."

Headmaster carefully held the ancient writings, "Before we begin, Hannah, please create a barrier of salt around the room.

Various cultures view the Anunnaki as gods of the underworld and others of the heavens. Today, there will be no history lesson. You can do the research and figure it out for yourself. Abadon is searching for this historical book of secrets to become the sole dictator in the universe. His thirst for power is endless, and his energy source is the chaos produced worldwide. Abadon is the personification of pure evil, known as the Destroyer. If there's such a thing as hell, he would have been the supreme ruler, said, Headmaster.

The book opened, revealing a medallion of pure white gold.

"Hannah, you have one like this around your neck!" Said Keira.

"Yes, like Hannah's pendant, this is a universal port key. There's no need to draw the power from the earth or the universe; it has its energy supply. Visualize your destination, and it will take you there. Who is brave enough to step out and gather the information needed to beat Abadon at his own game?" Asked Hannah.

Osric took Marion by the arm as she rose from her chair.

"Wait, I am not human, so if anything happens, I will be in a better position to escape from the hands of this evil tyrant."

Marion knew Osric was right. Her heart drops at the idea of anything happening to him.

Hannah picked up the enchanted medallion. "Look into the golden port key and see your destination."

Keira stood beside Osric and whispered. "You forget, cousin; I am not fully human."

Concerned looks observed as Keira and Osric entered Abadon's domain. They appeared as manikins sitting at the table after their life forces had left their bodies. With a wave of his hand, Headmaster placed a shield around their empty vessels.

The astral port transported Keira and Osric to a beach littered with human bone fragments. The air was dense with smoke, and the moon barely illuminated their route.

"Osric, the dark realm carries its name fittingly. What if someone were to set a trap?" Keira grumbled.

"It is better to be above ground."

"I can't feel my stone pulsating."

"We don't need our bodies in this realm. Abadon is an entity without a physical form. The only thing keeping us hidden is Headmasters' protective spell." Said Osric.

Approaching thunderous voices could be heard.

"Keira, quick, get on my back. Osric transformed into a black-winged stallion and flew through the clouds like the wind.

Keira looked down and saw a large gathering of Minotaur. "Osric, look, they have a bull's head and a man's body. What is this place?

"It is a place of deep darkness, where the degenerates and murderers of society receive their life sentences.

"I remember we spoke of this place before."

"It is the perfect place to harvest souls," Osric murmured.

"I'm so tired. I want to curl up in my bed and sleep forever."

"Keira, it's time to go home; I feel it too."

They came through the port key and re-entered their bodies. The book slammed shut.

"Visiting enemy territory was too dangerous." Said, Headmaster.

"We came across a large gathering of Minotaurs."

Hannah rose to her feet and waved her wand, creating a barrier.

"Returning to Raven's would give us an advantage."

"Your right, Devon; the villa has security measures that very few can enter. We leave in the morning."

"If we are to fight Abadon at Raven's House, he will need a human body," said Devon.

Hannah walked over to the wall safe, took out an old wooden box, and placed it on the table. "This medallion will prevent your divine spark from being drained by the evil ones and give you a way to escape should you come against something you can't handle. Until further notice, there are no classes. We will tell our students and faculty; that Raven House is under renovation for significant repairs. I must warn you; that each medal emits specific energy levels that can only be tolerated by those who remain faithful to our mission. Abadon will be sent back to his world if he tries to wear this medallion."

"Unfortunately, he cannot die. We can seal the demon in a pure iron and silver vessel, neutralizing his power. Marion, you gave Keira and Osric twin pendants similar to Hannah's. Do not remove your pendants for any reason." Said, Headmaster.

"Hannah, I am going to get this bastard." Keira scowled.

Osric took Keira's hand. "Let your sense of justice guide you, not hate or revenge."

No one slept well that night, expecting danger to strike at any moment. They all knew this would be the most challenging battle they'd ever faced.

TWENTY-SIX

MIRROR, MIRROR TAKE ME HOME

A young girl appeared in Keira's room, and her Aura was bright.

"How did you get in? I didn't invite you."

The child smiled so sweetly. "The evil one knows who you are, and he is coming for you. Take nothing for granted." Then she faded away.

Keira hurried to the dining room to find Devon and Marion. She stood still at the end of the table, waiting for an opportunity to speak. Osric got up from his chair to fill his serving bowls a second time.

"Keira, the child spirit is your protective angel."

"How did you know I had a visit from my guardian?"

"We all have the gift of telepathy, and your thoughts are roaring."

"Osric, remind me to cast a hedge of protection around my mind, body, and soul."

"The psyche is highly vulnerable to attacks. You were going to tell me about your visitor," said Osric.

"He's coming for me, the angel said."

"He is coming for us all. Instead of dwelling on the negative, let's do something different," Osric added.

"Would you like to go shopping?" I need to pick herbs for my mother."

"I'm not sure it's a good idea." Keira hesitated, thinking about the message she had received from her guardian.

"Go, Keira; the outing will be good for you. Hannah left early this morning and will not be back until after sunset tomorrow. Devon and I are going to be okay." said Marion.

They headed down to the village in the old pickup. The winding roads were full of potholes, and gravel kicked up, hitting the truck.

"Slow down, Osric. You know we have less traction on gravel roads. We should have used our medallions; this is horrible." Keira scowled.

"I can imagine the impact if someone sees us appear out of nowhere," said Osric.

"They need a truth serum to see through all the lies they have heard about witches and the supernatural."

"What is the point? Many believe we are nothing more than basket cases who believe in fairy tales."

"Keira, are you feeling okay? I have never seen you in such an aggressive mood."

"I am fed up with all this rubbish that is going on."

Osric was silent. He didn't know what to say to make her feel better.

They spent the afternoon going from one store to another. Finally, they decided to have pizza and a pitcher of beer at their favorite restaurant.

"Osric, I have not eaten this way in ages."

"I could have more," he said"

"The sun is setting, and it will take us at least an hour to get back home."

"Hold on to your medallion," said Osric.

The truck was at the front door in a matter of seconds.

"I feel sick," she said, clutching her pulsating stone.

"What's wrong?"

Dread covered Keira's face as she looked out the window.

"Osric, there is something off."

They walked into the house and saw Devon and Marion sitting in a stupor by the fireplace.

"Mother, are you alright? Osric asked.

Marion looked up to the ceiling and began to weep. Andria, Keira's mother, had a wooden spike pushed through her heart, hanging in midair.

Keira screamed. "Who did this? Aunt Marion, you said that there is no such thing as evil. Take a good look at my mother, and tell me that there is no evil.

"Keira, whether you come from Christian faiths or pagan traditions, evil and darkness are the same things. I do not have a reasonable explanation for what happened here today," Marion said.

Keira cradled her mother's lifeless body and placed her in Devon's chair. Marion took off her shawl and covered Andria's face.

"Our home is no longer safe. A foul-smelling entity held me back; I looked up, and Andria was hanging in midair, dead. We have a secure location in another realm. At midnight, we will use a unique port to get there." Said Marion.

Osric frowned. "What port are you talking about?"

Marion murmured, "You will find out when the time is right."

"Mom, are you sure about this?" Asked Osric.

"Please don't worry about it; I have this covered."

"Keira, we will enter a wormhole that leads to other worlds. I am not sure exactly where. My mother had no problem going in and out of these ports.

"Osric, the wormhole has a gravitational force that would tear us apart in seconds.

"We are not regular people. We can travel through time in the twinkling of an eye. Space and time will slow to a crawl for ten seconds at midnight, and we'll cross over safely."

The following day, Headmaster sat in the library and went into a trance. The sacred rod leaning against his chair morphed into a gold snake, slithered up his back, and wrapped itself around Headmaster's body. His power and knowledge were absorbed into the staff. Marion heard his voice calling her into the room. The royal scepter materialized in her hands.

"You know what to do; my time has ended," said Headmaster.

Marion entered the living room with the enchanted wand.

"Our mission has changed. Keira, Headmaster, has transferred all of his power to you."

"Aunt Marion, Headmaster said he would be with me forever."

"It is up to you to uphold the equilibrium in the universe. Keira, all you have to do is accept this royal office, and you will share his kingdom. This staff contains knowledge, wisdom, and power.

"I have been feeling odd lately. It is hard to explain."

"Keira, you are just a bundle of nerves. I am surprised that you have not had a burnout; you will not fail." Marion said.

The golden staff became like putty in Keira's hand, and it snaked itself around the top of her head. Boundless energy flowed into Keira's brain, altering billions of synaptic connections and creating new pathways in her brain. Keira fell to the floor, and Osric rushed to pick her up.

Marion raised her hand, "do not touch her; she enters a new dimension. She must unite with her spiritual guide."

Keira had an out-of-body experience and found herself standing in a cave with fire and molten lava spewing from every crevice. Terrified, Keira is ready to run. "Please, do not leave. This is not hell," said the creature.

"Who are you?"

"I am wisdom and pure magick. We can divide into two separate entities in this plane of existence." Said the being.

"You are so lovely. Your feathers are gold and silver, and your eyes are glowing red rubies. What is your name?" Asked Keira.

The creature looked into her eyes, and the mystical bird replied after a short pause.

"We are one, and we have a mission to complete.

"Keira smiled; we are one."

Her stone broke free from her heart and landed in the lava pit.

"No, my stone, I need it back."

"Stop! Spirit said firmly. "You do not need that gem. Remember, this stone was nothing more than your training wheels. Keira listen to me carefully. Can you hear the tortured souls, their cries of desperation and confusion? Dark opportunists prey on the surrounding worlds. They are crying out for our help."

Keira began to cry, and her heart shattered. "I cannot stand the screaming and the cries of anguish. It is cutting right through me. I never realized how much suffering there is in this world."

Spirit wrapped his large wings around her body, and Keira disappeared inside the mystical being. Still lying on the floor, Keira opened her eyes and whispered. "I'm so cold."

"Osric, help her up," said Marion.

"Keira, you look different. Your face is no longer one of innocence but maturity and wisdom." Osric said.

"I have gained the inner strength and knowledge needed to complete the task. But it is more than that; I know why I am here. I have to put an end to the madness."

"Madness?" Marion queried?"

"What better way to defeat your enemy than through fear and self-doubt? Therefore, a hedge of protection covering your hearts and minds must be in place," Keira said.

"That is the first lesson we teach our students at the Academy," said Marion.

"Keira continued. "Dark wizards have come together to create a secret society, and you will never guess who the founder is? Abadon!"

"Keira, stay here with Osric. I need to activate the hidden portkey.

Marion waved her hand and said, "*Speculum Magicka Nunc Videtis Nos. Nobis Donet In Patria.*"

An old mirror materialized at the main entrance.

"What did Marion say?"

"Keira, brush up on your Latin, mom said, *magick mirror take us home.*

"Osric, this mirror belongs to your grandmother Hagatha, and she is the most powerful witch who ever lived. She, unfortunately, preferred the dark arts and fled the coven. This mirror is like a time machine of hope. You are the architect of your future.

"Aunt Marion, how far ahead are we talking about?"

Marion smiled. "Keira, I would suggest the near future."

Keira sighed with relief.

Osric smirked. "Keira, what juicy bits are you hiding from me?"

"Too spicy for you," She whispered.

Marion positioned Osric and Keira in front of the mirror. "Once the clock strikes three thirty-three, walk through the mirror."

"Three thirty-three? Earlier this evening, you said midnight." Said Keira.

"Yes, I did say midnight, but now that our circumstances have changed.

In his flippant manner, he said, "Mom, it is a woman s prerogative to change her mind."

Keira shook her head and thought. "Osric, this is not the time for your remarks."

"Get it together, son. Lives are depending on us."

Marion's demeanor was grim, and Osric knew when to stop his juvenile behavior.

"Aunt Marion, I have chosen graduation week."

"Perfect. See you both soon."

> *"Life and death are illusions. We are in a*
> *constant state of transformation."*
> *Alejandro Gonzalez Inarritu.*

TWENTY-SEVEN

PERILOUS GATHERING

"Hey, Laurence, come in. I am just looking for the other shoe."

Keira slipped on her running shoes, grabbed her bag, and walked to the exam room.

"It is scaring the hell out of me. I have reached my late twenties, and I am still uncertain about my future." Said Keira.

"Really," said Laurence. "Are you one of those mature students? I would never have guessed it."

"Laurence, are you telling me that I look good for my age?"

"Of course, you are beautiful. Why do you think I try to cop a feel every day?

"Oh, shut up, Laurence, you never have."

"You are wonderful, Keira. Do not worry yourself sick. It will happen."

"Your right. I know my stuff."

Keira and Osric walked into the classroom and hurried to their desks. Mrs. Graven, a geologist interested in natural crystals, stood up in front of the class. She clapped her hands multiple times to cut through the chatter.

"Now that your midterms are over, this last exam will determine if you will graduate. If you fail today, you have two other attempts. Before we begin, I have a guest with us. He is a great man of science and magick. Next year, he will teach reptilian magick and its spiritual value. Please put your hands together for Professor Abadon."

Keira could not believe the monster had entered the school. The entire class got to their feet and greeted him warmly. Osric sat a few rows ahead of Keira and sensed her fear. Osric communicated with her through telepathy.

"What's wrong, Keira?"

"Osric, his father, tried to rape me, and he infected me with his dirty magick.

"Keira, you are not the same person. He cannot hurt you. Wanton returned to his realm when Samael destroyed the creature he occupied if I am not mistaken. Wanton's son, Abadon, is impersonating his father to confuse us. It is Abadon. You can send him home with one thought."

"You are correct, but I am concerned about the others. Abadon, like his father, has a distinguished appearance and is ready to pounce on anyone that enters his path."

"Stay calm; we will meet after class." Said Osric.

Abadon stood in front of the class and gave a formidable speech. His thinning hair gave way to an old demon. He is smooth and portrays a meek man unable to harm a living thing. Keira is disgusted with his deceitful performance. Keira finished her exam and left the room. She went through the back entrance to avoid being near him.

"Osric, did you see him. That snake." Keira said sharply.

"Keira, calm down. All that hatred will cloud your judgment. He is the reason that we are here. Where did he go?"

"He must have scurried back under his rock," Keira said.

Laurence came out of class and was excited about their guest speaker.

"What a charmer. Professor Abadon has invited our class to one of his lectures. Keira, are you going?" Laurence asked.

"Laurence, his father, is of the dark side, and what his father has done to me, Abadon, will do to you. He is dangerous."

It has been a while since Laurence and Keira spent time together. Their friendship drifted apart because Laurence is jealous of Keira's abilities.

"I do not want to hear any of your wild stories. Just look at this man; you must see how harmless he is? I will be attending his lecture."

"Laurence, do not be so foolish. How can you be fooled that way? Can you not discern by now that he is not human? What is your stone telling you?" Said Keira as she slightly tugged on Laurence's shirt.

Guilt-ridden, Laurence quickly backed away. "Leave me alone, Keira. Something tells me to get away from you before I belt you in the mouth."

"Laurence, I am afraid of what might happen to you. You are refusing to see the obvious." Keira shook her head and walked away.

"I am worried about him," said Keira.

"I did not like the look on Laurence's face when you tugged on his shirt. He left rather quickly and disappeared into the crowd." Said Osric.

"I am going back to my room to rest. I have had enough surprises for today." Keira said

Keira lay in her bed, planning how she could interrupt the lecture. Someone knocks at the door, interrupting her thoughts.

"Enter Osric. I knew you were going to check in on me."

"I thought you would like some company."

"Good, I didn't feel like being alone," Keira whispered.

Keira got out of bed and took her cookie tin from the dresser. Keira patted the bed and asked this beautiful creature to come closer. Osric morphed into a gorgeous male with ocean blue eyes.

"It did not take long for you to transform. Spend the night with me, and whatever happens, it is our secret."

"Are you sure about us tonight?"

"I would not have given you an invitation. Said Keira.

Keira walked into the library the following day and saw one of the young librarians flirting with Osric.

"Excuse me," Keira politely said.

Osric had a sheepish look on his face. "It is not what you think."

"I was just another booty. That is fine; I needed your company last night. Thanks. Keira replied sharply.

"You are thanking me for last night? Now I feel cheap."

Keira laughed. "It looks good on you. I'll see you tonight for the lecture. It takes place in this library at nine o'clock."

"Nine o'clock? That's a bit late for a lecture," said Osric.

Keira watched Osric befriend those pretty girls in the library and wondered if she could fall in love with a changeling.

Osric is waiting at her door. "Keira, are you ready?"

Keira ran out of the room. "Did you not hear me? I said yes."

Osric smiled. "Miss me?"

"Not at all. Osric, let's go; I do not want to be late."

They saw the custodian finishing up for the night on their way to the lecture.

"The library door is locked, cried Keira.

Osric is still pulling on the handle. "Most likely, it has been canceled."

"Hey," shouted the caretaker, walking quickly toward them.

"What are you doing here? It is late."

"Sir, was the lecture canceled?" asked Keira.

"Didn't you receive an email or a memo in your mailboxes?

The professor changed the time to six o'clock."

Osric brushed his hand over Keira's shoulder.

"It is not your fault; you tried to warn them."

"I thought we could change the future."

"It would not have changed a thing. Abadon has a protection spell around his devious plans; we could not have detected his next move."

"Of course, he did," said Keira." Spirit had a protection spell surrounding us when we entered the beast's domain."

"Tomorrow, we graduate and then off to the police academy. Now that we are not around, that monster will be free to do as he pleases." Said Keira.

"This is not Wanton. Remember, Abadon is an impostor."

"I keep forgetting that Abadon has taken his father's place, but he seems more cunning than his dad."

TWENTY-EIGHT

S O M B E R
G R A D U A T I O N

"Hurry, the graduation ceremony is about to begin," Osric uttered.

"How do I look? Never mind. I do not need one of your wisecracks today."

"You are beautiful. I mean it."

Keira smiled, "you are so handsome. Your mouth has that kiss me look."

They walked into the auditorium, and there was standing room only. Marion tapped the microphone to get everyone's attention.

"All graduating students, please stand on my right."

"What is Marion doing here?"

"This is graduation day. Our headmistress hands out the degrees," Osric murmured.

"We have to tell her about Abadon," whispered Keira.

Marion handed Keira a degree in International Law with a major in Criminal Psychology. While accepting her certificate, Keira whispered in Marion's ear.

"I need to talk. It is urgent."

Marion smiled. "Yes, I know. See you both tonight."

"You knew I wanted to see you?"

"We will talk tonight." Marion insisted.

Marion came out of the kitchen just as Keira and Osric entered the formal living room.

"I proudly chose the Bloodberry English China to serve evening tea to my new graduates," Marion said.

"Aunt Marion, how did you know that we needed you?"

"Do you think I would have left you on your own?"

"Laurence is missing."

"Keira, I know. Hannah is beside herself with grief."

"Abadon has taken Laurence and Erin."

"Mom, could you not change the recent events and destroy this snake?" Asked Osric.

"No. If I were to change the past, it would disrupt everyone's future, including yours. You may not have been born."

"We cannot sit here and do nothing."

"We can no longer detect their amulets. Laurence and Erin are either dead or have joined the enemy," Marion said.

Osric walked over to the fireplace and stoked the burning logs.

"That's it, and life goes on."

"Not quite, Osric. I cannot say anything more. We will see Abadon again soon. Wherever your journeys lead you, I will always be there. Osric, are you still wearing the medallion I gave you?" Marion asked.

Osric held the medallion firmly in his hands, "I never take it off."

"Good, hold on to the pendant, and when you feel it vibrate, say my name. I will hear you." Marion uttered.

"Why did Abadon come back on the day of our graduation?" Asked Keira.

"He is trying to cast a shadow over a day that should be a treasured memory because he cannot stand to see us happy," Osric said.

"He is playing with your minds."

"Anyone who can control others in that way understands the effects of black magick." Said Marion.

"I thought black magick was a ceremonial thing."

"Keira, there is no such thing as black or white magick. It is the unique state of being or thought characterized as black or white. What counts is the intention behind the magick that is sent. Energy is a vehicle that transports intent to its desired goal." Said Marion.

Abadon's magick is powerful. He is the personification of death. Whether it's a blessing or a curse, the energies he sends out will return to him three times." Said Osric.

"Another of Abadon's curses is to wear us down mentally. He does not realize our beloved Spirit has healed my inner wounds of abuse. That fool believes I am still lost, and now he is out to control me."

"You are his prime target. Abadon knows you have the wand." Marion said.

"Sadly, he sets a trap for your capture using Laurence and Erin as bait," Osric murmured.

"Abadon expects you to rescue Laurence and Erin. It is four o'clock in the morning; I doubt they are still breathing," said Marion.

Keira yawned. "I would not know where to begin. I met Wanton senior at a busy mall. Maybe, I should go undercover as someone homeless. After all, his victims were those whom society deemed as disposable assets."

Marion abruptly set her teacup down. "Do not be so foolish, girl. Abadon has anticipated your every move. You do not know the strength of his powers. Have you not learned anything in your classes? Use common sense, not emotions."

"Aunt Marion, I am not daft. What do we know about Abadon?"

Marion picked up a book from the library. "This will tell you what he is, but not the power he may have. If you don't mind, I'm going to bed."

"Sure, if you need anything, let us know." Said Osric.

"Something must be going on. Mom has never acted that way."

Keira searched all night for information that would help her defeat Abadon.

Abadon can morph into whatever serves his purpose and control our minds. I hope we are not related." Said Osric.

"Osric, we are going to confront a horrible being. Are you ready to do this? Abadon existed long before the Big Bang, when life had begun. According to this book of Ancient Knowledge, there is no history of his origin. Wanton took advantage of the chaos, created the illusion of fire and brimstone."

Scientists are developing new theories about how the universe has come to be."

"What's the Big Bang?" Asked Osric.

"In a nutshell, the Big Bang is a scientific hypothesis of how the universe began. About thirteen billion years ago, the world started as a small scorching force that caused the universe's rapid expansion. As a result, stars began to form, and here we are." They called it the Big Bang theory. As for the possibility that Abadon is part of your family, I doubt it. Remember, he is the master of illusions. This demon is more cunning than the last one we saw the dark queen destroy. The question we must answer is, what is he afraid of the most? The answer will lead us to his destruction."

"The sun is coming up, and I think it will be hot. Enough for now. It is shower time." Said Osric.

TWENTY-NINE

DIARY SECRETS

Keira accepted a position as a detective with the Los Angeles Police Department to bring about her dream of working with the less fortunate. Twenty-four grueling months of training as a Military Officer helped Keira control her flash temper and gave her a new appreciation for civilian life. While satisfied with her accomplishments, Keira continues to fight the genetic seed of darkness inherited through her paternal father.

Another sweltering day, with no central air in the offices. Captain Forrester's voice echoed across the intercom. "Detective Keira Wolf, come to my office as quickly as possible."

"Yes, Sir, I'm on my way."

For the last year, Keira's assignments are not career boosters.

Keira took the stairs from the second floor to the ninth just for the exercise. As she entered the captain's office, the stench of sweat and cheap aftershave sickened her.

Keira is standing at attention, "you wanted to see me, Sir?"

"Wolf, you are not in the army. At ease, detective." Said Adrian.

He leaned back in his chair, looking over his thin rimless glasses.

"Keira, how long have you been with the department?"

"Roughly eighteen months, Sir."

"I'm not sure if you heard the latest news. I received a memo, a warning, if you will. We have to cut back on personnel beginning in the New Year. There are rumors of possible layoffs."

"Lay off's Sir. I have never heard of any police department having to let anyone go. Perhaps they will cut the hours on quiet nights."

"Keira, the world is changing. You know the old saying, money talks. A homicide division in England needs a couple of detectives to assist with a critical mission. Their government believes that corruption has infiltrated the police department. Unfortunately, their previous detective has vanished. I am sure you would be a good fit with all your military training. Are you interested?" Asked Captain Forrester.

"Sir, if I accept this position, who would be the other officer?"

"Detective Osric requested you as his partner."

Keira smiled. "Where in England, Sir?"

"London, and if you decide that it is not for you, I cannot guarantee you will have a job next year. Let me know as soon as possible. It is an urgent assignment. The department will cover all moving expenses; as for your house, we will take care of it." Said Captain Forrester.

"Do not worry about the house. A member of my family will care for it

Keira was pleased with her life, but she still dreamed of the day when Abadon was dead.

Keira's head was spinning from information overload.

"Sir, thank you very much for this opportunity. When do we leave?"

"If it were up to me, you would have gone yesterday. Can you be ready in five days?"

"Sir, five days is not much time to get ready, especially if I have to work between packing."

Flipping through her schedule, Captain Adrian continued. "Your paid vacation time should be enough to organize your affairs and pack up for the move. Keira, why don't you take the day off?" Said Forrester.

Keira left the Captain's office mystified about how all this good fortune had fallen into her life without the use of magick.

"What a great boss." thought Keira.

No sooner had Keira left her employer's office; Captain Forrester made a call.

"It is done. I am sending Maxine two rookies with bigger training wheels to spin than the last guy. They are walking around starry-eyed, hoping to make a difference. Yea, I am a great believer in fairy-tale too." Said Adrian laughing.

Nervously, the man speaking to Forrester on the phone said. "Adrian, are you sure this time? Robyn almost caught us soon after he landed in London."

"They are brainless trainees. They will never figure out what is going on. Stop worrying, Maurice. I will see you soon." Said Forrester.

Just as Keira walked in, homemade pea soup and fresh bread from the oven were on the table. With a baffled look, Osric wondered, "you are home early. Are you feeling all right, Keira?"

"Well, I have some news about my meeting with the Chief and the possibility of work after the New Year. Osric, thanks for referring me. London England! That is huge. We are moving up in rank without having to take the exam. Not bad for rookies."

"We both know what that means? The fight is on. I forgot to ask Captain Forrester how long our stay will be in London," said Osric.

"I suppose for as long as they need us. We are leaving in seven days. Let's have lunch, and then we will start packing."

Seated at the foot of her bed, Keira flipped through the family album, remembering the long talks she had with her mom. There was a time when Keira's family was her support and a safe place to retreat from the world.

Keira, a private person, was upset with Devon for trying to console her when she did not receive an acceptance letter from the girl's NHL hockey team. He knocked and entered her room.

"Leave me alone," she hollered.

Devon picked up an old feather pillow from her bed and skimmed the top of her head. Keira grabbed the pillow out of his hand, stood on her bed, and had a pillow fight with her dad. They were both covered in feathers from head to toe and laughed hysterically. Marion ran down the hall and saw them both looking like chickens.

"Do not move." Marion began to laugh so hard she could hardly breathe. Devon's hearty laughter momentarily lifted Keira out of her sadness. Keira's eyes shimmered with tears, remembering how much she missed her family life.

"Osric, I am going out, said Keira.

"Where?" Would you like some company?

"Do not worry; I will be back."

Keira drove for hours and wondered if she would ever make it back from England. The possibility of becoming a casualty of the dark realm was always at the back of her mind.

Seven days of preparation had gone by quickly, and still, Osric and Keira had not finished packing.

"Hurry, Osric, we are going to miss our flight."

"Keira, our flight from Los Angeles to England will be grueling. Would it not be possible to use some of our gifts to appear in London right away?"

"We risk leaving our energy residue behind. Abadon does not need our attention. There is more to do."

Osric and Keira quickly made their way to the appointed terminal. The gift shops were overflowing with tourists buying souvenirs as though they could not get a better deal elsewhere.

The PA system blared. "We are now boarding for London, England."

Osric and Keira sat in the most uncomfortable seats.

"What happened to your medallion? It is not there." Keira whispered.

Osric unbuttons his shirt. "I never take it off. Where is yours?"

"Osric, you are sitting in the wrong seat." Keira stands beside him.

"What is going on? You were sitting beside me until I asked to see your medallion."

"Osric, people are staring at us."

Keira opened her shirt and revealed the medallion nesting between her breasts.

"Are you satisfied? I did not realize how spooked you were about this mission."

They arrived in London on a Sunday afternoon, and the airport was overflowing with travelers. Amidst the chatter and scurrying, Keira hears her name called.

"Miss. Wolf over here."

Two police officers are heading in their direction.

"How did you know who we were?" Asked Keira.

"We received an email with your photos, and we are here to take you home. I am Sergeants Zoe Lupu, and my partner is Sergeants Abbey Grose."

"Thank you for meeting us. I cannot wait to see our new home," Osric uttered.

After the introductions, Keira and Osric walked to the patrol car, expecting a speedy arrival. Their new home is an architectural masterpiece adorned with 4,000 square feet of beauty. The focal point is a towering floor-to-ceiling stone fireplace of Italian marble and Calais stone. Keira suite borders the epicurean kitchen, whose windows display majestic views that reveal the history of England.

They barely relaxed when they heard a knock. Osric opened the door, and a tall, red-haired lady held a colorful fruit basket.

"I am Captain Maxine Kozlov. Are you Detective Keira Wolf and Osric? Do you have a last name?"

With a confident smile, Osric continued. "No, Captain, I was not given the last name.

"How odd," she replied.

"Captain! Please come in," said Keira.

In her usual guarded tone, Captain Kozlov continued. "Welcome to England, detectives."

"Thank you, Captain," Osric replied.

With the prompt and reserved delivery of an officer, Maxine added, "you can live in this lovely house for the duration of your stay. Tomorrow morning, I need you both at the station at nine o'clock. Zoe and Abbey will teach you our protocols. The headquarters are in London, and you will report directly to me each month. "I anticipate that everything will go smoothly." Captain Kozlov explained.

"Yes, Captain," Keira replied.

She handed Osric a basket of fruit, splayed with flowers that exude a delicate aroma of cinnamon and coffee on her way out.

Maxine Kozlov was not someone you wanted to offend. Maxine'superior training and tactical abilities have earned her a place among the world's top intelligence agencies. In the American Counter-Terrorist Unit, she was among the operatives assigned to the Canadian hostage crisis. Her mission was to rescue high-ranking officers. A Lieutenant in the army, Kozlov, an American citizen, experienced a traumatic loss on her last assignment. Maxine could not use her radio, fearing sophisticated enemy scanners detecting their location. The officer in charge of the unit sent Maxine to a nearby underground command post to convey pertinent information regarding their situation and defensive position. Lieutenant Kozlov returned to find all members of her squadron dead and their mutilated bodies scattered all over the base. The only person not present among the deceased was the Captain. Devastated, she climbed into her jeep and headed back to the underground command post.

Maxine came across Captain Marshall and two other men leaning against an army jeep, drinking beer.

"Welcome, to a new world, Maxine," said Marshall.

Maxine, with her rifle and jumped out of the Jeep. "What do you mean, Sir, a new world?" "Maxine, we spared your life because I think you are one of us." Said Captain Marshall.

"I am not sure if I understand, Sir." Said Kozlov.

"It is all about money and power. As soon as we get back home, nothing is waiting for us. If we support the enemy, we will never have to think about money again."

Maxine was beside herself and could not contain her rage.

"Are you out of your mind? You killed all these men for money and power. These young men had families and gave up everything to fight for our country!"

"Come on, Kozlov, grow up. We have to look out for number one. Others are lining their pockets while we are out here risking our lives." Said Captain Marshall.

Infuriated, she pointed the M16 and killed his two companions at point-blank. As for Marshall, she blew his legs out from underneath him. He dropped to the ground in agony. Kozlov stood over him and placed the barrel of her gun deep in his mouth.

"This is what I do to soldiers who betray my country and kill the men and women who protect it."

Her gun went off in his mouth, pulverizing his head beyond recognition.

Shortly after her tour, she spent several years in a veteran's hospital for Post-traumatic stress disorder and depression.

Maxine earned a clean bill of health and received orders from the MI5, the British foreign intelligence service, to uncover and destroy terrorist cells. Unfortunately, due to officials taking bribes in exchange for not disclosing criminal activities, she cannot locate the insurgents. Currently, a detective is missing.

Keira and Osric went out to look around the yard when a car came to a halt in their driveway. A middle-aged woman with curly white hair hurried out of a black Malibu, carrying a red vintage ceramic baking dish."

"Hello, I'm Angela. My house is just down the road from you. Welcome to our neighborhood!"

"Thank you, Angela; my name is Keira, and this is my roommate, Osric. Would you like to come in?"

Politely declining, Angela added, "I have so many things to do. Here is a pot pie that we cooked this morning. Marc and I thought you would appreciate a home-cooked meal after such a long flight," handing Keira the earthenware.

Keira realized the speed at which news traveled in their community.

"This is a small town, and the word does get around." Angela traced concentric circles in the air with her finger.

"I'm off to see the caterer. This Saturday is Marc's fortieth birthday. I want to invite both of you as our guests. This is a perfect way to make new friends. See you then?"

As quickly Angela arrived, she left like a whirlwind. As dusk drew near, Keira enjoyed the stunning sunset while sitting in a cozy lounge chair on the lanai. Exhausted by her day, Keira fell into a deep sleep and woke up with the bright morning sun rising. Keira and Osric arrived early on their first day of work and were surprised to see everyone there.

Looking dapper, Dr. Chang, a burly middle-aged man with a short-boxed beard, dark brown eyes, and rosy cheeks, stood by the cooler. Constable Nigel Burns' a twenty-five-year-old, incredibly handsome and with superior intellect, sat at his desk frantically writing an incident report. With her long flaxen hair, ocean blue eyes, and shapely legs, Nancy, the office secretary, sat entering data. Sergeant Zoe Lupu stood by the window, reading over the last evening's report. With a Ph.D. in psychology, Zoe is excellent at her job. On several occasions, the Department offered to promote her to Chief. She turned them down and clarified that she was not interested in the extra responsibilities. Her partner Jena is a hairstylist with a creative touch. One person is missing. Sergeants Abbey Grose.

Nigel gave Keira his report, "We had another domestic disturbance. Mrs. Anita Pavlu stabbed her husband Tom in the shoulder with a hunting knife."

"Where are they now?" Asked Keira.

"The husband is in the hospital, and his wife is in a holding cell waiting for the judge tomorrow morning."

"Nigel, were you able to find out why they quarreled?" Asked Keira.

"According to Mrs. Pavlu, her husband has been unfaithful several times during their marriage. She is not taking it anymore. She shouted as we cuffed her,

"You bastard, this is the last time you make a fool of me!" Said Nigel.

"Nancy, find out why Sergeant Grose is not in this morning. Keira uttered."

Nigel interjected. "I received a call from Abbey late last night. His transfer came through for head office."

"Why was I not notified of this?" Said Keira sternly.

The staff in the office became silent.

"Osric and I have been posted here to take charge of this department. In the future, all business regarding this Bureau must come through us. Is that clear?" Said Keira.

The staff nodded and quickly returned to their desks. While Osric was out on a call, Keira sat at her desk and began to go through the drawers looking for a pen to sign off on Nigel's report. The bottom drawer was locked.

"Nancy, do you have the key for this desk?"

"Sorry, the last person who occupied that office always kept the key on him."

Keira pried the drawer open with a brass letter opener that she had held on to since she was a little girl.

"Never mind, Nancy, I got it opened."

Keira found a self-titled diary, Detective Robyn Nickels, expecting to find stationery. Aware of recent incidents in the last few months, she quickly flips through the Journal.

"What are you reading?" Asked Osric.

"I found Detective Nickel's diary, but a few pages are missing."

"Keira, what secrets will we find in this diary? Since our arrival, everyone has been quiet about what has been going on."

Keira fetched the portable fingerprint kit and lifted several prints from the front and back cover of the journal. Then she read aloud through the accounts that Robyn had documented.

December twenty-eighth, 2019: "Presently, I continue to sift through the evidence collected from the unsolved cases applying new investigative techniques to bring closure to the families."

Cold Case Re-opened: HOMICIDE # 49 - Reported by Detective Robyn Nickels.

On Tuesday, September eighteen, 2020, police responded to a call at one twenty am, and gunshots were heard near the highway, beach area.

Constable Marciano and Detective Robyn Nickels found two men with visible gunshot wounds to the head, execution-style. They were pronounced dead at the scene.

Image #1; Jeremy Ali, 26, wore a dark blue hoody with one horizontal white stripe. This hoody is missing.

Image #2, Kaufman Eller, 24. The second victim was found by Robyn Nickels wearing a light green hooded sweatshirt with the word "Eller" in large black letters across the front. The sweatshirt is missing

Bullets were lodged in their frontal lobe and removed with a sharp object by unknown persons. No shell casings were found on site. Undetermined caliber without cases.

2013 January third: Detective Robyn Nickels

"I received a call at four o'clock in the morning with a warning to back off."

January twenty-eighth, 2020:

Break-in at Detective Nickels house, and there were 13 dead rats in the Nickels bed."

February tenth, 2020: A sticky note was placed on my front door which said, As Mario Puzo once said, "Revenge is a dish that tastes best when served cold." Death threat!

Valentine's Day, February 14th: Detective Robyn Nickels. I had a heart-shaped box delivered to my front door, and I placed it on the counter after noticing the bottom of the box was a little warm. I discovered a human heart in a chocolate pie when I opened the box.

February twenty-seventh, 2020: Detective Robyn Nickels

"I received an anonymous tip this morning. A letter was delivered to the police department. It said, "There are items at the old gem mine that you may find interesting."

Later that evening, I drove to the excavation and entered a narrow entrance. The cave had wire-cased lights. Walking through the cave, I found human remains covered with the missing clothing that belonged to the shooting victims. While collecting the clothing as evidence, I heard someone coming down the passageway. Quickly I hid behind three large barrels of crude oil and waited until it was safe to leave."

"Osric, this was the last entry in his journal, and Robyn went missing shortly afterward."

Without delay, Keira sent the prints to the lab for identification.

THIRTY

THE   UNEXPECTED

"Osric, I am not fond of parties. Fair warning, I will give it an hour before I leave." Said Keira.

A timeless black cashmere gown with hand-beaded shoulder straps is among a few girly pieces of clothing in her closet.

"Not bad for a tomboy," Keira thought as she looked into a full-length mirror.

"I'm ready. I am eager to get this over with," said Keira.

"What has happened to the Keira, I knew? You are not wearing your black tuxedo?" Asked Osric.

"What is wrong with my dress? Is it too much?"

"Osric's eyes slowly scanned her body from head to toe.

"To the contrary, you look delish!"

"Cut it out; time to go."

Marc and Angela welcomed them with a glass of red wine. Keira shook Marc's hand, wishing him birthday wishes.

"I am forty, and I feel like twenty," Said Marc playfully, pulling his wife to his side.

Marc and Angela moved to England from Newfoundland, Canada, twenty-two years ago. Marc, an architect, designed most of the local residential communities in the area. His short stature did not prevent him from achieving his goals.

Although Angela is seven years older than Marc, she has a who gives a damn attitude about life. Angela ushered Keira and Osric through the dining room and introduced a few of her guests. Many were dancing and appeared to have begun celebrating a little earlier than planned. Keira felt slightly uncomfortable meeting everyone on a social level. She preferred a police officer's approach.

"Keira, I would like you to meet Leanne Guild, my neighbor. She manages our Outreach Center." Said Angela.

Leanne began the conversation with some local gossip, which did not interest the young couple.

"This is going to be a boring night." Keira thought.

Bill and Martha Stevenson, an older couple, are known to be party crashers. Mr. Stephenson, a loud and obnoxious man, has no qualms about prying into anyone's private life. Between his vast wealth and ego to match, Bill is shameless.

"Leanne, are you overwhelming our guests with a barrage of local gossip?" He looked around, hoping that everyone could hear him. The tension between them increased considerably.

"Excuse us; this is a private discussion, Bill."

"You obstinate witch."

"Are you upset because you could not get into my pants last weekend? That bonfire was not the only thing. burning hot." Said Leanne.

"Martha, do not believe that animal. She envies the upper-class lifestyle."

"Watch your mouth, pervert, before I tear your neck open and spit down your throat," said Leanne

Keira quickly interjected before someone threw the first punch.

"Good evening, Mr. and Mrs. Stevenson. I am Keira Wolf."

Bill continued with a raised eyebrow and a condescending retort, "Yes, I hear you're the new detective in town. Typically, we have men take on that sort of occupation. The women stay home and take care of their husbands."

Mr. Stevenson's cynicism is sickening, and Keira would not let that bigot's remark go.

Defiantly looking into his eyes, Keira replied, "Mr. Stevenson, I believe your attitude is well suited for the narrow-minded clicks around town. Unfortunately, many people get rich in today's economy by sucking the poor dry. Only a handful of women can afford the luxury of staying home."

Holding back her laughter at the mortified look on his face, Keira smiled.

"If I were independently wealthy, perhaps it would be an option. Besides, this type of conversation is inappropriate for this festive gathering." Keira smiled and walked away.

"Lady, who do you think you are?" Barked Mr. Stevenson.

"Easy Keira, we need allies, not enemies," Osric whispered.

"I could not help myself. It was either giving Stevenson something to think about or turning him into a sewer rat." Said Keira.

"Osric, since the beginning of time, the human male has recognized that he is physically more muscular than the female, resulting in a male-dominated society. The adage that men will always be at the center of the universe is long gone. Fortunately, today, women have equal access to independence and wealth.

"Keira, you are saying that men are evil."

"Of course not. I have many male friends who admire women for who they are and do not consider the female gender as the weaker sex. I refer to corporate bullies who believe that you must be a man to accomplish something meaningful. This philosophy of male dominance is seen all over the world.

Grrr, I should have been a politician and ran for President. Unfortunately, numerous women believe that lie. As long as we're on the topic, how many women have been President? Do not get me started, said Keira.

"Keira, Mr. Stephenson, is an older man, and in his generation, society had different standards. I know that men are leading most of today's businesses. The idea of a woman doing their job is threatening their ego. This type of mindset will not change overnight. Sure, male executives will say that women should have equal rights if their position is secure. There will be a balance of power. It has already begun. Women all over the world hold executive positions held by men.

"Eat something; you will feel better."

"Emotional eating, No, thank you." Said Keira.

The chefs came out of the kitchen with steaming roast beef, pork, sweet potatoes, salads, and homemade bread. They also had a lovely spread for vegetarians and vegans.

Walking through the living room, an older gentleman with a sympathetic face, gray hair, and a mustache gestured to join him. In a soft, French accent, he introduced himself. "Bonjour, I am Maurice Champagne. I am happy to make your acquaintance." Are you a good friend of Marc and Angela?" Asked Maurice.

"We met Angela a few days ago," Said Osric.

"So, are you new in town?"

"Yes, we have taken new positions as Detectives." Said Keira.

"Congratulations, I hope you will like it here. My daughter and I are from Montreal. We have been living in England for twenty-eight years. I met my late wife Cynthia here, and our only child Marissa is teaching at the local university," said Maurice.

Nearby is a handsome man with curly black hair in his late thirties and a wisp of gray feathering his temples. He was listening to Keira's conversation. He lowered his blue eyes so as not to appear intrusive. Taking the initiative, Keira smiled, nodding in his direction.

"Keira, what are you doing? Are you asking for trouble? He may come from the dark side." Said Osric.

"We will never know if we do not make the first move. Osric, I am just playing the game. How are we supposed to break through the barriers? Stay close."

"Do not be so sexy, Keira." Osric snapped.

"Are you jealous? You do look a little green."

The young man confidently walked over and stretched out his hand." I am Laurier Chandler."

"Pleased to meet you, Laurier," Keira said.

"Laurier, do you work in London?" Asked Osric.

Laurier appeared anxious. "I am an anthropologist.

"What are you working on?" Asked Osric.

"The National Museum of Natural History has commissioned me to determine if ancient customs can be relevant in today's society."

"Is this for the Smithsonian? Keira wondered.

Laurier nodded.

"How interesting. Your work keeps you busy, I'm sure," said Keira.

"What do you do, Keira?" Laurier asked.

"Osric and I are from Los Angeles, and we are the new detectives in London."

Laurier walked over to the buffet table, and Keira noticed his limp.

"Laurier, I am not trying to be nosy, but what happened to your leg." Asked Keira.

"I suppose you are more discerning than most. I will write it off as an investigator's curiosity. As I walked through the forest, I fell into a hole meant to capture a large animal."

The music began to play just as Keira was leaving the table.

"Keira, dance with me before you go. I may not see you again."

Keira struggled to look interested in their polite conversation, and she understood that acting vulnerable would help her objective.

"Would you like to have lunch with me someday? My schedule is wide open," said Laurier.

Keira smiled. "Call the office, and perhaps we can go for coffee."

Looking over his shoulder, Keira spotted Nigel at the front door.

"Laurier, excuse me for a moment; Angela would like to speak with me."

Nigel is standing in the entrance hall with a sad countenance.

Keira had reactivated her gifts and knew something was up.

"What's wrong, Nigel?"

"Detectives, we are needed."

"Can't it wait until tomorrow? We are celebrating a friend's birthday."

"Sir, a dead body has been found by a local."

Keira and Osric thanked Angela for her hospitality and rushed home to change.

They arrived at the site and entered a government-owned apartment complex. Ramsey, an older man in his late seventies, greeted them. He began to describe what he saw on the first floor.

"On my way out, I walked by the open door and saw that poor girl lying there. It was just horrible."

"We are going to take it from here. Thank you very much for your help." Said Osric.

Ramsay walked away, shaking his head. "This world is the mirror image of hell."

Everyone waited in the hallway until the forensic team had finished processing the scene. Pictures of all rooms have been taken from every angle. A boom overhead camera took pictures of outside buildings, exits, and spectators.

The forensic team finished their work an hour later, and detectives entered the crime scene. Nigel's knees became weak at the sight of blood.

"Sorry, but I can't handle this," said Nigel.

"Nigel, interrogate the neighbors and see what you can find out," said Keira.

The apartment appeared to have been searched, leaving it in chaos. A straw-colored handbag sat on the floor near an umbrella stand. Osric emptied its content on the kitchen table and discovered a weathered black wallet.

"The victim's identification read: Cassandra Suarez.

"What a waste of life," Osric whispered.

Keira examined the area where the body lay and saw a large pool of dark-red blood spreading outward from the underside of Cassandra Suarez's body.

"Osric, this might be blood, or it may also be decomposition fluid, which resembles blood at a certain stage. I will leave that mystery to the coroner."

"Her throat was slashed with great force. Whoever did this was very angry," said Osric.

"Keira, take a look at this. Cassandra's head is barely hanging on. What kind of person could do this to another human being?"

Blood splatter covered the walls, including the ceiling. The weapon was never found.

The coroner had just arrived at the crime scene with a mask covering his nose and mouth.

"Dr. Chang, her name is Cassandra Suarez. Could you give us the estimated time of death?" Asked Osric.

"As a rule, the core body temperature drops at an estimated one and a half degrees each hour. But it will vary depending on the surrounding temperature, humidity, movement of the air, and fat levels in the body. There is a thin cloudy film that has developed over the eyes. It usually happens within 3 hours after death has occurred. The eyes become softer due to less fluid pressure, which helps with the time of death," explained Dr. Chang.

Keira continued. "Dr. Chang, it is eleven fifteen. Would you say the time of death was between eight and nine-thirty this evening?"

"Yes, Detective Wolf, this is the best estimate I can give you."

While driving home, Cassandra's mangled body kept rushing through Keira's mind. Over the last six months, Keira has worked on several crime scenes but nothing like tonight.

Osric and Keira sat at the computer and researched what kind of person could commit such vicious crimes. There was one particular site of interest.

Biology and environmental maltreatment increase a person's chances of becoming a violent criminal. According to Dr. Adrian Raine, a neurocriminologist at the University of Pennsylvania, the amygdala is damaged in psychopaths' brains, which is the most noticeable difference. This is the portion of the brain that controls our emotions. Keira searched for her notebook in the old trunk that Marion had given her to review what she had studied in the field of criminal psychology. She found what she was looking for, a dissertation on the different types of psychopaths.

The first type is distempered psychopaths. They generally have had a sudden outburst of rage, unassailable sex drives, and obsessive sexual compulsions. They also yearn for excitement, such as kleptomania or pedophilia.

Keira started to tremble as she continued to read.

Osric put his arms around her. "We don't have to go on."

"I have to overcome this anger," whispered Keira.

Osric continued. "Then there are primary psychopaths; they will not respond to stress, punishment, or disapproval. They have no goals for their lives, and they exist without emotion, good or bad. Another powerful feature is that they do not understand the meaning of words and phrases. In other words, they don't feel anything.

Flashbacks of her screams went unheard as the word NO rapidly left her lips. Keira could no longer hear any more. She began to be restless and rage-filled her whole being. She had awakened a dark and wrathful creature from the past.

Exhausted, Osric was just about to lay his head on the pillow when a strange scraping noise came from the lanai.

Keira stood behind Osric, "Do not move! My hound may get angry."

Keira took a second look at Osric and realized that he was the black dog in her dream. Osric returned to his original state.

"You should not have gone back to human form. Now he knows."

"You did not see that," Osric said.

"Anyway, if you did tell anyone, they would believe you are a person who is not playing with a full deck," Keira said.

"I need your help. I am detective Robyn Nickels."

"We have been looking for you. Do you have identification?" asked Osric.

"The department picture ID and my badge are in my back pocket."

Keira instructed Robyn to place his badge on the coffee table.

Having verified his credentials, Keira invited him to the kitchen for coffee.

"Robyn, if you do not mind, your body odor is terrible. Take a shower, and I will give you some of Osric's clothing to wear, then we can talk."

Said Keira.

"The bathroom is to your left." Said Osric.

"I will call Captain Kozlov and tell her that you are safe."

Robyn followed Keira and Osric into the living room and sat comfortably in front of a large bay window. Keira walked over to the cherrywood wall unit and picked up a voice-activated recorder to capture their conversation.

Waving a small recording device in her hand, Keira continued. "Robyn, would you mind if I record the information.

"No problem; I have plenty to say."

Robyn began to tell Keira about his long journey when he saw a white van pulling up in front of the house. The vehicle's side door slid open. Three men wearing bomber jackets and carrying assault rifles jumped out. Robyn knew his time was up. He grabbed Keira and Osric and threw them on the floor. The bay window shattered, and the walls riddled with bullet holes. The assassins climbed back into their van and sped off.

Osric used his body to protect Keira. As she rose from the floor, blood trickled down her face.

"Keira, you have a nasty cut," whispered Osric.

He placed his hands over the wound and said, "I promise, no scars."

"You are full of surprises."

Robyn lay face down a few feet away with several bullet holes in his back. Osric checked for a pulse.

"Robyn is dead. He never had a chance to tell us what happened to him. Now what?" Said Osric.

Neighbors began to gather in front of the house, wondering what had happened.

Police cruisers arrived within minutes.

"There is no need to check for vitals. Robyn is dead," said Nigel.

"Nigel, how do you know he is dead if you have not physically checked for a pulse or breathing?" Asked one of the officers.

"His color is bad."

"His color is bad? Remind me to appoint someone else to check my vitals if anything happens to me." Said the young officer."

"Officer O'Connor, I am not a rookie," said Nigel

Keira looked around the room with horror.

"Someone knew that Robyn was here tonight."

"Keira, what are you thinking?"

"Osric, we have someone that is playing both sides. Who have we told about Robyn's sudden arrival?"

"You are not suspecting Captain Kozlov. Are you?"

"It's either the Captain or the person working for the answering service. At this point, nothing would surprise me." Said Keira.

Osric continued. "Keira, you are trembling."

"I can no longer live as a human being. I could have saved Robyn's life," said Keira.

A stranger walked in carelessly, disturbing the evidence that might have led to a suspect. Coldly, Agent Curtis Rosado, a distinguished twenty-year veteran with the Secret Service, introduced himself.

"Detective Wolf, I am agent Rosado; this case is under our jurisdiction. I understand you were in charge, and we would appreciate any information you may have."

Keira is relieved to know that help has finally arrived.

"Detective Robyn Nickels had information that could have been relevant to this case," said Keira

Curtis continued to question both Osric and Keira in search of answers. "Did detective Nickels hear or see anything that would suggest that he had discovered evidence of criminal activity in the area?"

"Robyn died before he could tell us anything at all. There's no point asking any more questions; we have no information. Said Osric."

Curtis looked down at the broken glass and the spray of bullet holes that covered the entire room and said, "I will call you tomorrow with my report."

"That is it?" Asked Osric?

Without saying another word, Curtis smirked and left. Chills went down Keira's spine as she watched him get into his car and pull away.

THIRTY-ONE

CLOSER THAN ANTICIPATED

Reporters gathered in front of the police station, wanting to find out what had happened. To appease everyone's curiosity, Keira prepared a brief statement to avoid the probability of mass hysteria. She waited to speak until there was complete silence.

"As you have heard, three unknown gunmen fired at my house. Unfortunately, one of our colleagues died in the line of duty. As more information becomes available, we will keep you updated."

Reporters went wild with other questions shortly after Keira had finished her statement.

"Please, Nancy, get the captain on the phone," said Osric.

"I am right here. I understand you have faced some difficulties, "said Maxine.

"How did you find out so quickly?" Asked Osric.

"I came in earlier this morning to escort a few dignitaries to a luncheon. As I pulled out of the parking lot, I heard an emergency call to your home address on my car radio.

Keira interjected. "Detective Nickels is dead."

"You could have been a casualty, but the gunmen were not after you. Detective Nickels must have known too much about the organization," said Captain Kozlov.

Frustrated with all the secrecy, Keira boldly continued. "Captain, unless someone tells us what is going on here, we cannot do our jobs."

Captain Kozlov closed the door behind her. "What I am about to tell you must be kept in the strictest confidence. We have a pilot standing by to fly you home if you decide to leave. I will not be disappointed if you decide this transfer is not what you expected. You would be leaving with generous compensation pay."

Keira is troubled by Maxine's remarks about going home so soon.

"Captain, do you think this situation is for a more seasoned officer? Or you might want us to leave the country. Which one is it?" asked Keira."

Keira intuitively knew Captain Kozlov was not the person she portrayed.

Maxine let on to have their best interests at heart.

"Keira, I am concerned about the well-being of my team, and I am doing my best to prevent any fatalities on my watch. Criminal activity in Los Angeles is similar to what we are dealing with in London. However, at this time, we are investigating the possible dismantling of our renewable energy plants."

"I have heard about biodiesel in America, "said Keira.

"Good, you have some knowledge about this new energy source, and it will be worth Billions if we can get it off the ground. Enemy bombers heavily damaged the petrochemical sites during the war. Due to privatization, there is a monopoly on fuel prices."

"Osric interjected. "This is all about oil vs. biodiesel?"

"England does quite well in oil production. Why, Biodiesel?" Asked Keira.

Maxine continued. "I believe it is due to high prices, and not everyone can afford it. Construction sites are trashed, and workers are afraid to return to work. Whoever is doing this has the ability and resources to succeed.

"Captain, do you have any idea where to begin?" Asked Keira.

"All I know is; that many countries are adopting this technology and making a fortune. Sadly, someone is trying to stop the project in England.

"Is there a suspect we can interrogate?"

"Keira, the evidence collected is either missing or corrupt. There is a traitor in the department.

"Osric, please do background checks on whoever works for this office. From now on, we are working together." Said Maxine.

"Captain, I was told by agent Curtis Rosado that the FBI is taking over this case." Said Keira.

Annoyed, Captain Kozlov Said, "Curtis? Aka Rod Spooner. He is wanted for gun-running and murder in the United States, Britain, and Canada. He preferred the spoils of organized crime."

"I understand what we're dealing with," Said Osric.

"The Rosados are linked to an international crime syndicate. It seems that prostitution and human trafficking are major money-makers. They are the worst psychoneurotic and bloodthirsty family around. The secret service provided Spooner with tools to outwit our sophisticated technology for years. His specialized training makes it difficult to find him."

"Captain, Robyn, received an anonymous tip leading to the volcanic mine. An elite entertainment club just above the cave." Said Osric.

"Osric, please find out who owns the club, and I will meet you at the office before I go home," Maxine uttered.

Captain Kozlov drove back to the detective's house to look around. Workers were busy replacing a new bay window when Maxine pulled up. She spotted a shiny object near the walkway where the white van had parked. A metal knuckle knife lay in plain view. Maxine carefully secured the blade into an evidence bag and placed it into the trunk of her car. Pleased with her discovery, she headed back to the station.

Meanwhile, Osric sent a text message to Maxine regarding the joint ownership of the club. Chief Adrian Forrester and Maurice Champagne owned equal shares in this lucrative business. Osric immediately called the Los Angeles police department to speak with Forrester. The receptionist informed him that he had retired several weeks ago.

Sergeants Lupu arrived early for her evening shift.

"Zoe, please send this knife to the lab immediately and fax the results to my private number."

"Captain, I still have thirty minutes before my shift starts," said Zoe.

"Zoe, I will give you ten seconds to do what I asked, or you will not have a job to come back to."

"Yes, Mam, right away."

"Captain, did you receive my text on Forrester and Champagne?"

"Yes, tomorrow morning, we will drop by the club. There is nothing else we can do tonight. Keira, I booked a room for you and Osric at the Gold Leaf Hotel, and this is where you will stay until the repairs on your house are completed. Go home, both of you, and get some rest. Drinking espresso for the last twenty-four hours will take a toll on you.

Osric and Keira entered the hotel lobby, and the atmosphere was warm and inviting.

They followed the baggage handler to a large suite and placed their suitcases close to the bed.

"Quaint little room," said Keira.

A queen-sized canopy bed with matching nightstands, dresser-mirror, and armoire were handmade from natural oak.

"Osric, I thought the Captain had us in separate rooms. Can I trust you to behave?" Asked Keira.

With a sheepish look, Osric continued. "If it bothers you that much, I will morph into a kitten and sleep on the couch."

"Stop with the guilt trips. I' will order another bed."

Osric smiled. "I guess you do not trust yourself with us sleeping in the same bed."

"Let's not go there, Osric."

"Oddly, we have become so busy with this case? Are we being deterred from our original mission?" Keira wondered.

"We are led in the opposite direction. Only a being from the dark realm knows we are looking for Abadon."

"Your right; my sixth sense has been screaming at me all day," said Keira.

"The secret of life is honesty and fair dealing. If you can fake that, you have got it made."
Groucho Marx.

THIRTY-TWO

ROMANTIC INTERLUDE GONE WRONG

With just a few hours of sleep, Keira and Osric managed to drag themselves out of bed and hurried to have a bite to eat before their shift started. Keira spotted Laurier as she entered the dining room.

"Good morning," said Laurier.

"Likewise. Do you mind if I sit with you?" Asked Keira.

Pleasantly surprised, Laurier stood up and pulled out a chair.

"Of course. I called your office several times, but you did not return my calls.

"Did you change your mind about having coffee?"

"Laurier, there was an incident, and one of our colleagues has died. Detective Nickels, who has been missing for several months, arrived at our house last night. He was in the process of explaining where he had been for several months, and suddenly we were shot at by three men. Robyn tried to protect Osric and me from their line of fire. Sadly., Robyn was killed. We're staying at this hotel until the repairs on the house are finished," said Keira.

"Yes, I read about it in the morning paper. I am sorry to hear about your colleague. Is there anything I can do?"

"Thanks, but everything is fine for now."

"Keira, I stay here for the next two years or until my work is done. You know how it is. Government cutbacks from one year to another can change my life in a flash, leaving me standing in the unemployment line at any time. Anyway, enough about me. We should go out for dinner."

"Sure, providing nothing comes up that needs my immediate attention. Osric is working the night shift. I would appreciate the company."

"I will meet you in the lobby at eight o'clock tonight."

"See you then," said Keira.

Maxine was still on the phone trying to get an arrest warrant when Keira entered the office.

"Captain, I couldn't help but wonder, for whom is the arrest warrant issued?"

Handing Keira the report, Maxine continued. "We have received the lab results.

"Forrester's fingerprints are on the knife used in Cassandra Suarez's murder."

Keira was disappointed to hear the news but not surprised. She remembered Adrian's reaction to her inquiry about the missing detective.

"Captain, where is he now?"

"The evidence is leading back to the club. We will need back up." Maxine uttered.

Keira parked the unmarked car under a tree, casting a shadow over the vehicle that made it almost impossible to detect.

Captain, I recognized that man. His name is Maurice Champagne, and the girl must be his daughter Marissa." said Keira.

Keira and Maxine entered the building with two officers. Maurice greeted them in his usual cheerful manner.

"Bonjour, Detective Wolf, how good to see you again. Captain Kozlov, it has been a while since we have spoken. Will you be having dinner with us?"

"This is not a social call. We are looking for Adrian Forrester," said Keira.

His smile faded. "Adrian is not here at the moment. When he returns, I will have him contact you."

Maxine smirked, "How well do you know this man?"

"Captain, as I said, Adrian will contact you," Maurice replied tensely.

It was clear that Maurice was not going to reveal his whereabouts.

"If you speak with him, tell Adrian to come down to headquarters to answer a few questions," said Maxine.

Maurice gave Maxine a warning stare and walked away without saying a word.

On their way back to the office, Keira was angry with herself for not being a better judge of character.

"Captain, I should have known that something was wrong with Adrian.

"Where was my head?"

Surprised by Keira's outburst, Maxine continued. "Do not be so hard on yourself; they are hardcore criminals. They can charm a hungry dog away from his bone."

"I do not understand, Captain."

"Keira, they are related to the underworld bosses, and the plan is to continue their family's legacy. There is good money to be made in arms smuggling.

Because of Robyn's outstanding work, we are closer to a conviction. Keira, I would advise you not to go out tonight and be alert." Said Maxine.

The newly-organized crime syndicate is still in its infancy. Robyn managed to infiltrate Forrester's operation a year ago. Champagne ordered him to kill members in their organization for not promptly showing up when called. Murdering this man would have sealed his allegiance. Robyn knew his time was up, and they would be hunting him down like a wild animal. Detective Wolf and Osric have an advantage that others never had. Like their predecessors, they would have to learn their trade through trial and error.

Keira was exhausted from her day and decided to make it an early night. She called Laurier and canceled their date. However, he was not dismayed by the change of plans. Laurier ordered room service and arranged for an evening meal in her room. Keira is unaware of his intentions.

She removed her clothes and took a refreshing shower to help release the day's tension. Warm water caressed her face, cascading down her back. There is a knock on the door. "Just a minute, please," Keira called out.

Osric saw the busboy holding a large silver platter through the peephole.

"Are you sure you have the right room?

Laurier appeared behind the attendant. "I hope you do not mind; I thought Keira would appreciate a little food after a long day at work."

Osric was not pleased with this man's tenacity. "Laurier, that is inconsiderate of you, especially being told that she was too tired for visitors."

"Leave him in." Said Keira.

"Laurier, I was not expecting you." Keira shivered in her bath towel.

Osric gave Laurier a dirty look and hurried to fetch Keira's housecoat. Keira accepted his thoughtful gesture. Un-impressed by Laurier's trickery, Osric grabbed his jacket and rudely said, "time for work

Keira and Laurier sat on the love seat, eating their late dinner. Laurier switched on the stereo, hoping for a romantic evening that neither of them would forget. They danced slowly, taking in the atmosphere.

Keira felt his warm breath against her neck. His hands moved down to her hips.

"Laurier, I am sensing you are up to something."

"I want you, Keira. It would be a perfect ending to our first date if we were to spend the night together."

"How do I get out of this? I do not want to hurt his feelings. Then again, he is not interested in me personally, just a good time." Keira thought.

"Laurier, have I given you the wrong impression because of the bathrobe?"

"Oh, Keira, It's just a little love. No harm in that. Is there?"

"No, Laurier, it's not about a one-night stand. Friendship is not about sex?" Said Keira.

Keira hoped he would understand without being offended. Keira sat down, and the awkward silence sent the message that she was not interested.

"Sorry if I've misled you. I need a friend, so let's enjoy each other's company.

"Laurier, you should know I am asexual."

"Stunned, Laurier was at a loss for words.

"I rarely experience arousal. I can have a romantic relationship, and I will keep my partner satisfied when needed.

"No hard feelings. Let's have another beer and toast to our new friendship." Said Laurier.

The sound of their crystal beer mugs coming together chimed in a new relationship, and they talked until the witching hour had passed.

Morning broke with the sun glaring in Laurier's face.

"We spent the night after all," he chuckled.

Before Keira could respond, Maxine called with a critical break in the case.

Keira jumped off the couch and headed for her closet.

"Laurier, I am needed at the station. Call me later."

He let out a sigh. "Could we not have a quick breakfast together?"

"Please do not expect more than I can give you." Said Keira.

Laurier rolled his eyes and said nothing more about it.

Feeling sluggish from last night's drinking, Keira jumped into the shower. Laurier quietly climbed in behind her. Keira turned around and was startled by his presence.

"Keira, please, before you say anything, you have no idea how much it turns me on knowing that you are asexual.

"Get out, Laurier. Now you have gone too far.

Laurier could have been an imposter. A beast from the dark side. Keira pushed him out of the shower.

"You have a lot of nerve coming on to me like that. I am not a piece of meat."

Laurier smirked. "Okay, I got it. You are not interested."

"Do not get so defensive. It' is not like you are half-demon, are you?"

Laurier's face dropped. "Half what? You are too weird for me. It is getting late. See you later, maybe."

Laurier left quickly without saying goodbye.

THIRTY-THREE

THE ENEMY HAS RETURNED

"You look chipper this morning, said Osric.

"I had a little sunshine for breakfast."

"Are you trying to make me jealous again? You are not glowing, and that is a dead giveaway."

She smiled, "you know me too well."

"Keira, this case has come to a dead-end. Forrester is always one step ahead of us," said Maxine.

"Well, there is a problem somewhere."

Maxine picked up the phone and called in a highly respected Profiler with thirty years of expertise.

"Sean Lawson will be meeting with us in a few hours. He will provide a profile on Forrester that will help us stop this nightmare."

Keira felt the darkness in her rising like a dragon stirring from a deep sleep, ready for the hunt.

"Maxine, I need some air."

"That is fine, but do not forget our meeting with Lawson."

Keira left the office. A transport helicopter was heading in the same direction on her way to the mine. Parking the car at a safe distance, she cut through the trees and hid behind the bushes. Men in bomber jackets unloaded the drums from the helicopter and moved them inside. Keira waited for everyone to leave before going back to her car.

Keira took pictures with her cell phone as evidence that Forrester was still involved in whatever they concealed in the drums. Within an hour, everyone had gone. On her way back to the car, Keira was hit from behind and knocked out cold. When Keira woke up, one of Forrester's employees was staring down at her.

"Hey Junior, she is awake. Are we still waiting for the boss?"

"He is busy right now. Shoot her if the girl gives you a hard time."

"I bet you are a sweet little thing." Said the older man.

"How long have I been out?" Asked Keira.

"About two hours. It is almost supper time, and everybody has gone home."

"What's your name?" Asked Keira.

"Why the hell do you want to know my name?" You will be six feet under in a little while."

"Leena, before I bury you, I will burn you alive." Said Keira.

"Who told you my name?" It doesn't matter; I will kill you before anyone finds out."

"Do your buddies know you are a hermaphrodite?' There is no shame in it. From 1500 to 1 in 2000 infants are born that way," said Keira.

"Drake," Leena called out, "come and keep an eye on her; I have a take a piss."

Keira recognized Drake from the wanted posters faxed to the office every morning.

"You are one of those serial killers who love to brutalize your prey before snuffing them out of their misery.

"I am a sick bastard and proud of it. I like the way you look right now, tied up, and legs all spread like that. I bet you are a juicy little morsel."

Keira lies on the ground, bound to tent spikes with her arms and legs wide apart.

Drake begins to cut Keira's jeans off and slowly rip her t-shirt open.

"I haven't had a gorgeous little thing like you in a long time."

"Sadly, you never will." Said Keira.

"Dream on bitch. You look too good to ignore."

Drake stood up abruptly, clutching his throat, and black smoke came out of his mouth. With incredible strength, Keira pulled all four spikes out of the ground and impaled his hands and feet, holding him firmly to the ground. Drake cooked from the inside out. "Internal combustion is too good for this man." She thought.

Keira closed her eyes and held her pendant, and she appeared in her room in less than a second, donning a fresh pair of trousers and a white tee.

"Keira, I have been trying to call you all day." Said Osric.

"I went for a walk in the woods and then became lost. My car had vanished by the time I discovered a way out."

Osric whispered. "You are expected to use your medallion to alert me. You are not telling me the whole truth, Keira?"

"Look, the amulet is still hanging around my neck, which means the light is still in me. Osric, let's not talk about this anymore." Said Keira.

With a message in hand, Nancy entered Keira's office. "Nigel is not in today. His message is barely legible, which is unusual. He said, "Sorry, away for the day, back early tomorrow morning. Nigel."

Keira stared at Nancy like she was looking through her.

"Detective, are you okay?" Asked Nancy?

"What time did Nigel leave the office last night?"

"I am not sure, roughly six pm."

Keira rose from her desk and entered Nigel's office, looking for Robyn's missing diary pages. She sat in his chair, and her eyes swept the entire room. Keira asked herself, "where would I hide my dirty little secrets? Perhaps in plain sight?"

A lamp sat on the corner of Nigel's desk, and Keira discovered an opening at the base. She peeled away the felt covering, and several pieces of tightly rolled paper fell out the bottom.

They were the missing pages of Robyn's journal.

September 12

"At twenty-three hundred hours, I walked around the building and saw large barrels brought into the building through a loading bay. An attempt on Keira Wolf's life is planned shortly after her arrival. Members present at the meeting are Adrian Forrester, Maurice Champagne, and Constable Nigel Burns. The purpose of this discussion is to move weapons out of the country. Adrian said something else, but I could not hear him. Forrester seems to be in charge, while Maurice appears to be his assistant. Nigel is an informant who intercepted incriminating evidence that could jeopardize their scheme. Cassandra Suarez has been a member of Forrester's group for three years and managed prostitution in England. She decided to opt out of the criminal lifestyle. Sadly, death is the only way out. Adrian Forrester said he would deal with her according to organizational protocols."

"Why didn't Nigel get rid of this diary? He could have been wrestling with his conscience."

Keira finished reading just as a transmission came through. It was the lab results. She quickly picked up the report and began to read it.

Keira gave Captain Kozlov the missing page from Robyn's journal.

"I believe this will answer all of our questions."

"Nigel is the traitor. I understand why there has been little progress for the last year."

"We will discover who runs the organization tonight," said Maxine.

Sean Lawson arrived at the station at nine pm. He sat at Keira's desk and began to give details on how he came to his analysis of Forrester.

"Ladies, profiling Adrian is a waste of time," said Sean. He paused and opened a manilla folder.

"Adrian knows every ploy in the book to avoid being detected. Our team discovered that he has connections with terrorist groups all over Europe. We need to work longer hours to cover our basic living expenses in this failing economy. We have access to money, drugs, and nightwalkers with no moral compass. Ruthless thugs will take advantage of any situation, especially those struggling financially. Sometimes police patrolling the streets are enticed into certain situations that are hard to ignore."

"In other words, corruption is everywhere." Said Keira.

Sean continued, "Forrester accepts bribes in exchange for not reporting drugs, prostitution, and whatever else is going on. Be careful when you are out there looking for him. He is a murderous psychopath who repeats his crime with escalating brutality. His love for money, women, and the nightlife are his weaknesses."

"He spoke with such conviction against the drug trade in Las Angeles. I have forgotten how charismatic a psychopath can be." Said Keira.

"This is a steep learning curve for all of us. Adrian sent you here because he believed it was safer to have someone who does not have investigative experiences. He was not aware of your gifts."

"What do you know about my gifts?" Asked Keira.

"That night, I witnessed your handy work in the women's detention center. I did not bother reporting it," said Maxine.

"Why not, Captain?"

"Honestly, Keira, who would believe me?"

"What gifts?" asked Sean.

Keira quickly replied. "You know, a woman's intuition.

"Sorry, I don't believe in Mediums." Said Sean.

"Yes, and now it's time to show him who he is up against. How do we outmaneuver someone who has been on the force for thirty years? In our neighborhood, police corruption is on the rise."

Captain Kozlov yawned as she picked up her jacket. "Tonight's questions can wait until tomorrow. It's time to go home."

"That sounds good to me," said Keira.

"Would you like to go out for a drink? It should help us unwind," Maxine suggested.

"I have a better idea. Why don't we have that drink at my place and order pizza," Keira said.

"That's a better idea."

"Sean, would you like to join us?" Asked Keira.

"No, thanks, it's getting late. My wife would not understand why I should be drinking with two beautiful women?" He said.

Keira smiled. "Next time, bring her with you."

Keira picked up on Maxine's look of relief when Sean declined the invitation.

"I saw that look in your eyes. Is there something I should know about Sean?"

"Keira, Sean is a great person, but it's been too long since I had a girl's night out."

Maxine and Keira walked to the hotel, only a few minutes away. A black Limo drove up to the sidewalk, stopping inches away from Keira. The door opened, and Adrian stepped out of the car. With a condescending tone, Adrian spoke, "I hear that you're looking for me, ladies."

Captain Kozlov sneered. "Yes, Mr. Forrester, we need to answer a few questions. Would you like to follow us back to the station?"

"Captain, I am sorry to disappoint you. At the moment, I have a pressing engagement. Perhaps another day."

"Adrian, you must have struck oil. This limo is much different than that beat-up old heap you were driving in Los Angeles, said Keira.

"By the way, Keira, those were very nice moves in the lumber yard today. Now that I know what you can do, you are worth more alive than dead," said Adrian.

"What is he talking about?" Asked Maxine.

"He is a pathological liar, trying to cause trouble," said Keira.

"I have underestimated you. You are smarter than you look. Did I not warn you to keep the peace and mind your own business? No more warnings, you insufferable witch."

Knowing she could crush him like a roach, Keira continued. "Is that a threat, Adrian?"

"More than a threat Keira, if you don't back off."

Adrian's eyes became dark and menacing.

Keira smirked, knowing she would irritate the hell out of him. "Adrian, you may call me Detective Wolf, and you are right about me. I am a witch and a wicked one!"

"I can't believe the arrogance, knowing there's a warrant for his arrest," said Maxine.

They walked into the hotel lobby, and Laurier was making out with the receptionist.

"Relax, it is all right. Maxine and I are having a girl's night out. We are ordering pizza and forgetting about our slim figures. Laurier, that gorgeous brunette you are giving tongue to is full of surprises." Keira said.

Laurier smiled. "And your point is?"

The Receptionist quickly interjected. "My name is Clara, and my breasts are real, honey. As for the other parts of my body, it is a work in progress."

Clara, keep up the excellent work. Said Keira.

Taken by surprise that Clara was not a complete woman, the look on Laurier's face was one of devastation.

Indifferent about Laurier's prowess, Keira winked and said, "have a great night, love."

"Why not," said Laurier, "love is love."

Keira and Maxine sat on the couch in matching silk nighties, eating pizza, and drinking cold beer.

"Keira, are you married?" Asked Maxine.

"No, marriage is not for me. My life is full. And you, who is the special person in your life?" Asked Keira.

"My partner and I have gone our separate ways. Working long hours puts a strain on my social life."

"Maxine, someone will come along and accept your lifestyle." Said Keira.

Maxine grinned as she slowly moved closer to Keira. "Your blue eyes are driving me crazy. You can tell me to back off. Am I making you feel uncomfortable?

"Not at all," said Keira.

"I have been attracted to you from the first day we met." But I promise my feelings are separate from my work," said Maxine.

"I do not feel uneasy at all, just curious. I didn't know you were gay."

"My preference is for men. But what's a little pleasure between friends? We satisfy each other, and then we go back to our regular lives."

"Maxine, be careful; you may get hurt one day or hurt someone else. I do not mind if you spend the night, but nothing more. Besides, my heart is still on the mend."

"I am a little disappointed, Keira. I feel rejected. Just kidding. Where am I going to sleep tonight? Perhaps I can curl up on the carpet." Said Maxime.

"Do not be so silly; you are safe with me," said Keira.

The following morning Osric knocked on the bedroom door.

"Time to wake up, ladies. Breakfast is on the table."

Maxine shyly whispered, "Osric, nothing happened between Keira and me. It would be most appreciated if you did not tell anyone that I slept here. According to departmental policies, dating employees is not allowed."

204

"Captain, you can trust me. Not a word. I do not think that is very important right now." Said Osric.

Keira walked into the kitchen and saw Osric in a strange mood.

"Did you have another jealous fit because Maxine spent the night? What is it now?"

"Keira, we had a call from Nancy. It is Laurier; the maid found him dead in his room."

"How did he die?" Asked Maxine.

"The medical examiner said it was asphyxiation. Keira, you are white as a ghost."

"I think we know who is back," said Osric.

"Laurier and I spent the night together, but nothing happened between us. We fell asleep in each other's arms sitting on the love seat. I barely knew him," said Keira.

Keira and Maxine arrived at the office before dawn, working out different scenarios to arrest Adrian.

"Keira, I have got an Idea. We're aware of Forrester's sexual proclivity. Let's throw a toga party at the club. Our young recruits will pose as students."

That morning Keira sent the youngest team member to book a hall and finalize the arrangement.

"Maxine, he will not know what hit him," said Keira.

Osric took Keira aside and whispered. "Why all this scheming? With your powers, you can arrest Forrester without anyone's help."

"Osric, there is something more going on; Headmaster will tell me when to strike."

"It is not about finding a home so much as finding yourself."
Jason Behr

THIRTY-FOUR

LAST-MINUTE DETAILS

Captain Kozlov stood at the podium, adjusting her microphone, and she appeared to be nervous.

"We have divided you into groups. Please rise, Group One."

Twenty of the most attractive women stood up and were chosen for a particular assignment. Group one will engage in conversation with everyone in the hall.

"Do not be shy, ladies; you must be persuasive. Be a tease. Your togas are made of thin cotton."

One of the young ladies raised her hand.

"Yes, Sabrina, go ahead."

"Captain, how are we seductive without looking obvious?"

Keira interjected. "Sabrina, reach over the table for a drink or drop something on the floor. I am sure you will figure it out. However, make sure it is in Adrian's direction when you bend over. We must distract him. It may be an elaborate scheme just for one man, but he is wanted for one of the largest smuggling rings in the country. Adrian and his men will get physical. Of course, do what you can to avoid them, and your performance must be flawless. I understand this is asking a lot of you. A full backup will be waiting outside. When you hear the fire alarm go off, leave the building and retrieve the weapon from your vehicle. If anyone wants to back out, do not show up. Be ready, and

I will see you tomorrow night at twenty-hundred hours," said Maxine.

Keira received a call from the contractor, letting her know the house was ready.

"Finally, I get to sleep in my bed tonight," Keira said,

Maxine frowned, "I will post some men around the house until this ordeal is over."

Keira and Maxine entered the house, and the smell of fresh paint was still lingering in the air.

"The Police Department remodeled the entire house just for a bay window and a few walls?" Keira said.

"Robyn was the last person to live here," said Maxine.

Constable Jeffery's called out from the kitchen. "Detective Wolf, you need to see this. I believe you may have a secret admirer."

On the kitchen table stood a large Silver vase with twelve beautiful red roses. The card isn't signed. Suspicious of the anonymity, everyone knew this was not a friendly gesture.

"Trash them," said Osric. "The roses may be poisonous or worse; they may have absorbed a dark and deadly spell."

"Sir, isn't that going overboard? Magick is not real," said Jeffreys'

"Just because you do not believe it does not mean it is not real." Said Keira.

Keira took a warm shower while Osric made dinner. Halfway down the stairs, she observed a woman sitting on the couch.

"Do not be alarmed. It is just me, Keira."

"Hannah. What are you doing here?"

"The time is coming to fight this battle once and for all. I know about your toga party, and so does Adrian."

"We were so careful about any of our plans falling into the wrong hands."

"Your office has been bugged. Keira, you will need your enhanced powers, regardless of who may see them," said Hannah.

A smile appeared on Keira's face. "Finally, I can be myself again."

Marion came out of the kitchen with a large serving bowl of Italian ravioli. Maxine followed with a hot garlic cheese breadbasket.

Keira leaped from her chair, pleasantly surprised. "Aunt Marion, I am so happy to see you."

Marion chuckled. "What a lovely welcome. I told you we would all be together one day."

"Sorry to put a damper on this joyful reunion, but we need a change of plan." Said Osric.

"What happened to my little jokester? My son has matured," said Marion.

Osric smiled if you say so, mom.

"We'll need a soundproof barrier before starting this meeting," Hannah said.

She drew concentric circles in the air with her wand, and the room was bathed in white light. "Done."

"Keira, your father, is spirit, and he was able to infiltrate Adrian's meetings."

"What do you mean, Hannah, by spirit form?"

"Devon had a massive heart attack, and by the time the ambulance arrived, he had passed on. Your father is still part of the team. He is, however, no longer burdened by a human body.

"Are you telling me my father is with us?"

"Of course, he is. The human body may die, but the spirit lives on. Later, you can bring him back, but we need Devon in his present form for now," said Hannah.

"Aunt Marion, you know some people do not think there is anything like ghosts."

"Keira, we know there is a spirit realm and supernatural gifts. If someone chooses to close their minds and deny that there is nothing more than this natural world, it's on them," said Marion.

"Where do we go from here?"

"Osric, the office has been bugged. We need another strategy, said Marion."

"Maxine, you are quiet. Do you have questions about what you have seen or heard here tonight?" Asked Osric.

Maxine shrugged her shoulders. "Not at all."

Hannah knew something was not right. Maxine's aura was dark and unstable as if someone were sharing her space.

"We need to sweep the office as soon as possible." Said Keira.

"We do nothing," Maxine whispered. Our strategy must unfold as planned."

"I do not expect Forrester to be at the party. Hannah, what did my father learn?"

Hannah's eyes became hard. "This story about biofuel plants going up in London and crude oil imported for public consumption is only part of the story. Bioweapons containing deadly airborne viruses will be launched from England's borders and cause a pandemic like the earth has never seen. England's Secret Intelligence Service, also known as M16, has been misled. The antidote must be purchased and injected within thirty-six hours, or death will be imminent."

"What if a country becomes infected and cannot afford the cure?" Asked Osric?

"Well, my dear boy, they all die." Said Marion.

"It is not hard to figure out. It has all the markings of the Dark Lord." Said Keira.

THIRTY-FIVE

T O G A   P A R T Y

Maxine, you are in early this morning," said Keira.

"I did not sleep all night. I had a recurring nightmare."

"What about?" Asked Keira

"The bloodshed I have witnessed on my last mission. I do not want to talk about it."

"I hear you. I am no shrink, but I understand how severe PTSD can be.

Irritated, Maxine continued. "I don't like the inference of the word. Are you implying there's something wrong with my head? People like you don't know what it's like to lose a part of yourself in battle."

"You're right, Maxine; I don't know what you are going through. I'd appreciate it if you didn't bite my head off because of my ignorance." Said Keira.

Maxine deliberately changed the focus of their conversation to ease the tension that arose between them.

"How was your first night home?"

"I slept like a baby."

"Keira, what if Adrian comes after you?"

"It is too soon for another attack; besides, I can handle him."

"Now that your gifts are activated, you seem pretty sure of yourself."

Keira smiled. "It is best if we do not bring up my ability."

"Tell me, why are you so mysterious?"

"I will never speak of my gifts. If the enemy knew what to expect, it would give him leverage."

"I have letters to mail. I will see you later," said Maxine.

Osric observed Maxine arguing with someone on her phone as she slowly pulled away.

"Maxine is not herself today."

Osric sat by Keira, took out his wand, and created a soundproof barrier.

"Keira, it is time to activate the powers Spirit passed on to you."

"I am afraid of what I might do."

"If you're not up to the task, you should delegate your duties to someone else. I don't want to be insensitive, but we need a leader who will not be afraid of her own shadow. This is war. Expect casualties." Said Osric.

"Are you calling me a coward? I am trying to avoid killing innocent people. I have killed out of self-defense and felt no remorse."

"Keira, listen to yourself. You did nothing wrong. The keywords are self-defense. Adrian is not the man you once knew; he belongs to the dark realm."

"Osric, how do you know all this?"

"Adrian gave up his career and his family for power and wealth. He is not the type to throw everything up to chance. I cannot prove it, but I am sure Samael had something to do with it before you defeated her. We installed microphones in critical hall areas and placed firearms in the recruit's vehicles. Was it all for nothing? Keira, we must change our strategy. We are running around in circles."

"Osric, you heard what Maxine said; we are not changing our preliminary plans."

"So, what are we supposed to do? Stick around the club while Forrester is getting ready to infect the world?"

"Please trust me. I have seen the results, and be ready for the unexpected; that is all I am asking. As for Maxine, she will lead us straight to Forrester."

"Keira, are your powers restored, asked Osric.

"I knew you would figure it out, but I see you are out of sorts today. What is wrong?"

"Since we were shot at in our home and Robyn killed trying to save us, I am afraid something will happen to you."

"Osric, we have to take life as it comes. No matter what, I will always be there for you. Our recruits will be arriving soon."

"Keira, I am sorry for calling you a coward. I misjudged you."

"I am not a coward, just cautious."

The Disc Jockey played the latest tunes, and the party was in full swing. Salads, hamburgers, pizza, and non-alcoholic beverages were available at the buffet tables. Maurice sat at the back of the hall, watching the girl's toga dancing. He was captivated by their sensuality. Occasionally, the girls would look back at him and bend over. Dina, a member of the kittenish group, had gone a little too far. She propped her leg up on a chair and bent over to reach for pizza. Dina revealed more than her thong. She felt warm hands on her buttocks. Surprisingly, she kept her cool. Dina slowly turned around with a sumptuous grin, looked into Maurice's deep brown eyes, and said, "That feels good. Let's keep it for later when there are not so many people around?"

"I will be waiting." He said.

Shortly after this unexpected incident, Maurice received a call on his cell and moved to another room for privacy. Dina ran outside to find Keira sitting in an unmarked car. After explaining what had happened, she was sent home for her protection.

"I know where to find Adrian. He is somewhere in the tunnels." Said Keira.

"How do you know this? I think he is hiding in the club." Maxine insisted.

"I tell you what, you search the club, Osric, and I will cover the tunnels."

Maxine was upset by the sudden change in her plans. "I am in charge, not the other way around."

"Sorry, Captain. I just wanted to catch this man so badly. No disrespect intended."

With a sigh, Maxine agrees. "Go ahead; I will follow and watch your backs."

They entered the tunnel through the loading docks, ready to confront Forrester. Osric came through the front entrance with back up. The undercover agents retrieved their weapons and detained Adrian's men.

Adrian could hear the commotion above him and ran further into the tunnel, eager to reach his boat at the riverbank; Keira intercepted him.

With contempt, Keira said, "at one time, I wanted to be like you.

I was so nervous in your presence. As a young novice, I wanted to be as competent as you were. Now, you make me sick."

Keira motioned to one of the officers to take him out of her sight.

Keira and Osric made their way to the upper level of the cave located just beneath the club and interrupted an arms delivery.

Osric was ecstatic. "Keira, we hit pay dirt. Look at all of that state-of-the-art weaponry and surveillance equipment."

Keira flipped the cover off one of the barrels. She found the biochemical substance that could kill millions if they did not pay up.

"No way, Osric, this poison is the prize. What we have in this container is VX, a nerve agent. The only antidote for VX is the combination of HI-6 and atropine.

"What is in this second canister?" Keira wondered.

"Ebola is an airborne virus, and the only treatment is Regeneron (REGN-EB3) and mAb114. Unfortunately, it is not a cure. It is a treatment that may or may not work."

"I hope that's all there is." Said Maxine.

"Both VX and Ebola are insanely expensive to produce, not to mention the resources needed to move the chemical into the biosphere. I doubt there is more." Said Osric.

"Maxine, I will stay back." Keira stayed behind as the officers led the smugglers into the police van. She instinctively knew there was something more going on.

"Keira, please do not put yourself in danger. I will call for backup."

"Not this time. There are no laws in my realm." Said Keira.

Ten empty barrels stood against the wall. One of the lids appeared to be moving. Keira slowly removed the top and discovered someone hiding in the drum. Keira backed away and pulled out her gun.

"Show yourself," Keira commanded.

To her surprise, there stood Curtis Rosado. "Get out of that barrel and slowly lie down face to the floor."

Keira quickly placed her cuffs tightly around his wrist. She activated her radio, ready to report her findings when Rosado spoke.

"My father enjoyed his playtime with you. As I recall, you were a feisty little girl."

"What did you say?" Asked Keira.

Arrogantly Rosado continued. "I am sure not many people are aware that your father relished selling you to the highest bidder for a bottle of whiskey."

"You did not do your homework. Francis was not my biological father."

"But he was still a drunk," Rosado said, laughing.

Flashbacks of her childhood began to play out in her mind. Keira's eyes became black as coal, and years of absolute hatred rose from the pit of her stomach.

"You must be so uncomfortable with your face to the ground that way?"

With just a flip of her wrist, Rosado was seated against the wall.

Fearfully, Rosado continued. "Keira, that is quite the trick."

"Samael and I enjoyed watching you struggle to fight my father off. We wanted to break your spirit. Pity, we failed that night. We did not expect your familiar to be there protecting you. That black creature was intimidating."

Rosado laughed at the disgusted look on Keira's face.

"Do you have children? You should invite me over to dinner one night." Said Curtis.

His handcuffs unlocked.

"We are going to have so much fun together." Keira said with sexual inference."

With a sultry and evil stare, Keira removed her medallion. She slowly unbuttons her shirt, slightly exposing her bosom. "Will this do for now?"

She slowly walked toward him.

"Closer." Curtis insisted.

"Curtis, tell me what you want, she whispered.

"Keira, I can smell your perfume. Come closer."

He was now in a sitting position, which made it easier for her to finish the last part of her therapy.

"Come much closer; you excite me. I knew one day I would have you."

Keira walked toward him with a small pistol that materialized in her hand.

Curtis's breathing became heavy. He closed his eyes, expecting her soft touch. He felt the cold steel of her gun right between his eyes in its place.

In a seductive voice, Keira whispered, "I have forgiven you and your father for all the pain and torment you have put me through at a tender age. However, I can see you have not changed. Is your father alive?"

Curtis looked up at Keira, and with hesitation, he replied. "He died several years ago in prison. You must understand, my father controlled me," said Curtis, terrified.

"Was it your father's fault for the gratification you experienced while I suffered? Curtis, your father, died when the brass letter opener plunged into his neck. You confessed that you and Samael enjoyed watching while your father tried to molest me. I was a real source of entertainment for you. Changing your story will not save you now. See this gun, Curtis? It is too good for you. I must protect my future children from all sick degenerates like you. I have a great responsibility to protect the public against individuals born without a conscience."

Keira hears a voice thundering through the cave. "Keira, pull the trigger."

"What are you doing here?" Keira screamed.

"Keira, end the nightmare. You have the strength and power." Maxine bellowed.

"Oh, Maxine, I have something better waiting for Curtis than a bullet."

Fearing for his life, Curtis pleaded with Keira to spare him. Keira feels nothing.

With deliberate intent, Keira sat beside Rosado locking her arms around him.

"Keira, your body is hot. Are you sick? Move away; you're burning my skin."

Curtis' feet caught fire. This incinerating fire gradually destroyed his entire body. His shoes melted off his feet, and his flesh fell away from his bones. His screams while being burned alive were horrifying.

Keira lifted her hands into the air and said. "*Amice, terra et ignis meus voco. Celare me factum.* My friends, earth, water, wind, and fire, I call you by my side to hide my deed, so mote it be."

The ground shook. Thick black clouds began to form and moved over the cave. The old cave floor opened its mouth and swallowed Curtis's burnt remains, making it his permanent home. Keira buttoned her shirt and walked out of the mine.

Maxine gulped as she spoke. "Keira, did you cause the cave to implode?"

"Maxine, it happened for a reason. After Curtis was burnt alive, my last thought was, how will I explain this chard body? With just a few words, the next thing I know, the earth swallowed him up. Maxine, you were so curious about my abilities. Now you know what I can do."

"I can't put this in my report. No one would ever believe me. Keira, there were no witnesses and no shots fired. You know how to cover your ass. My report will say; that an earthquake was the cause of death."

"Maxine, you look disappointed." Said Keira.

With a forced smile, Maxine walked away.

Keira drove home from the office late that afternoon with such satisfaction as she replayed the day's events in her mind. She pulled up in her driveway and noticed the lights on in her house. Slowly Keira opened the door, and the smell of steak and onions lingered in the air. She walks into the kitchen to find Osric and Marion preparing lunch.

"I cooked your favorite meal," said Osric.

Marion served a T-bone steak, medium rare, baked potato with sour cream, and baby carrots fresh from the garden.

Keira enjoyed every morsel on her plate. She lifted her head to speak to Marion and saw Abadon sitting in front of her.

Keira got up abruptly from her chair, furious to see this demon in her house.

"Where are Marion and Osric?" Asked Keira.

"Do not worry about them. Out for a stroll, I imagine. Keira, I am a great impersonator.

"I have had a trying day. You're lucky; my senses didn't detect you sooner," said Keira.

"I have my trusted shield around me. There is no way you could have detected my presence."

"I am grateful that we are enemies. Daily you teach me how to protect myself from your trickery. How did you get in here?" Asked Keira.

"I had one of my minions deliver flowers before you arrived home that evening. The contractor presumed that we were a legitimate business, and they took the flowers. Remember the silver vase of roses when you entered the kitchen. Osric threw the flowers but not the jar. I was the silver vase," Abadon said.

Keira shook her head, upset that she had not decerned his presence in her own house.

"Did you think cooking a meal for me would bring us closer? That is what your father thought when I was just a little girl. He is dead, you know." Said Keira grinning.

"Is he Keira?"

"What brings us closer is the depth of evil you are willing to accept into your life. The deeper you go, the more intimate we become. You were so wrapped up in the hatred and bitterness for Forrester and Curtis; that you did not detect an intruder in your house. Soon we will be partners and become the personification of evil."

"You are wrong, demon. I am destroying evil, said Keira.

Abadon threw his arms around Keira, and once again, her body became a ball of fire.

Abadon whispered in her ear. "Keira, let go of your essence and enjoy every moment we have together. Soon it will be for eternity."

He slammed Keira into the wall. "Ah, you bitch, do not burn this body; I still need it."

Keira grabbed onto her medallion. Within seconds Osric appeared beside her.

Osric took a few steps toward Abadon. "Do you think you can come here and take what you want?"

Keira grabbed Abadon by the throat, turned him around, and pinned him against the wall. "Where are Laurence and Erin?"

Abadon laughed. "As for Erin, she has chosen to serve a higher purpose. Laurence will be the mother of my child in just a month from now. Life is good, Keira, and it can be for you too."

"How can Lawrence have a child? He is a man."

"We are supernatural beings, and we can use any vessel we desire."

"Get out, you monster. Now! Do not come back here." Keira shouted.

"Keira, why didn't you kill him?" asked Osric.

"I need to find Laurence. Perhaps, we can save him."

Osric continued. "Laurence is infected. There is nothing we can do."

"Not too long ago, I was diseased, and my professors saved me. Maybe we can do the same for Laurence."

THIRTY-SIX

BREAKING THE ENEMY

Keira sat in her favorite chair and began her daily meditation. Terrifying images flood her consciousness with visions of Laurence screaming in excruciating pain. His body splits open, and a copious amount of blood is soaking the bed. Laurence's voice began to weaken, then silence. His pale, stricken face, eyes wide open, and battered body lay still as Laurence exhaled his last breath. A cloaked figure picked up the baby and left quickly. Keira's heart was racing from this horrible vision. She quickly made her way down to Osric's room.

"Time to get up. Breakfast is ready," Keira shouted.

Osric opened the door. "Would you like to come in"

Ignoring his usual nonsense, Keira continued. "Hurry, there is work to be done."

Everyone enjoyed a good old fashion family breakfast. Usually, someone is missing.

"More tea, please," said Keira.

Osric spoke with a mouth full of French toast. "What is the big hurry this morning?"

"Osric, "I raised you with manners. Did I not?" Said Marion.

Embarrassed by his mother's reprimand, he replied sarcastically.

"Yes, mother, it will not happen again."

"I need to get married and move out of here." Osric thought.

"I heard that," said Marion."

"Stop reading my mind, mother, or I will be graphic."

Marion shrugged her shoulders. "I'm sure it's nothing that I haven't seen before."

"Aunt Marion, while meditating early this morning, I saw Laurence passing away in childbirth." Said Keira.

"I know all about it. Hannah is on the offensive. I've never seen her like this before. Stay out of her way until her rage subsides. Laurence was simply an incubator for this imp, and thankfully, there is no genetic link between the child and Laurence. It's a complete demon." Said Marion.

"I hope we find Erin in time before she meets the same fate as Laurence."

"Keira, we haven't heard from Erin. She may be lost forever. Within twenty-four hours, that baby will become an adult. Abadon knows if we travel to his realm, our life essence will be drained, rendering us defenseless. We wait until he comes to us." Said Marion.

Marion is concerned about this next meeting with the evil one. Keira will be facing her first real battle, and this time, her courage must not falter.

"Keira, I have special daggers enchanted to kill fiends, but you must plunge the knife through their hearts or cut off their heads."

"Aunt Marion, these are the most powerful weapons ever made."

Not knowing how many to expect, Osric decided not to take any chances.

"I have called in a few re-enforcements. Hannah and your father are joining us," said Osric.

"Keira, heavy snow is sticking to the glass as if someone is deliberately trying to keep us from seeing what is out there. We are in mid-July. Do you think anyone will notice? Said Osric.

"I do not like this at all. What if I lose it and destroy every being in one sweep?

There will be humans among them," said Keira.

A voice came from behind her. "You will not fail, and together we will succeed."

"Dad?" said Keira. She leaped into his arms and began to cry.

"I have missed you so much. I need you now," said Keira.

"I'm here for my girl, and now, no more tears. We must pull together because the time is close. I received some intel this evening. The new mistress of the underworld will be making an appearance tonight."

The enemy is after something much bigger. He's out to control all realms."

Hannah walked into the dining room. Keira could not believe how evil she appeared. Her look was stern, and her eyes were like burning coals. The emotional impact of Laurence's death had taken its toll on her. Hannah lifted her dagger and said. "We will end this tonight."

The oil lamps began to shake, and their flames went down to a low burn. The house became cold as ice. "I can smell them, pure sewage," Hannah remarked.

Devon and Osric walked into the sitting room. "Ladies, we have company." Said Devon.

Hannah and Marion are ready to fight. Keira managed to smile and appeared relaxed and confident.

"Who do we have here? Nice to see you again, Maxine. I suspected you were one of them."

Maxine smirked. "It was a last-minute thing. I got a better deal."

"Like what? A new car?" asked Keira

"I was offered eternal life and wealth beyond my wildest dreams. Finally, all that I desire is at my fingertips."

"Everything gets old after a while, Maxine. What happens when boredom sets in?"

"I will let you know when it happens."

"There is a price for everything. And one day, your boss will collect it. In a last-ditch effort to save his life, Rosado told me who that mole was. You wanted him dead so badly because you knew he would sell you out to save himself," said Keira."

"Forrester, have you lost your way? Coming into this house could be fatal to your health. Oh, a man with few words," said Keira.

"Shut up, witch. Tonight, I will finally enjoy watching you draw your last breath. Sending you here was a big mistake. You interfered in my most lucrative plans, and I lost some serious money," said Forrester.

"You thought I was that stupid?"

"I still think you and your little friends are a couple of morons." Said Forrester.

Two women in black silk cloaks stood behind Maxine. Large hoods hid their faces. The first person took a few steps forward and removed her covering.

"My name is Celina. You may have known my carrier, Laurence."

Celina looked into Hannah's eyes and smirked as she walked away.

"You bitch. I am going to kill you." Hannah cried out.

"And who are you supposed to be? There new mistress?" Asked Keira.

The hooded stranger was much taller and walked proudly. In an arrogant demeanor, the peculiar woman said. "I hear you have been looking for me. Well, here I am. It is so cute; you were worried about my wellbeing, touching."

She removed her hood and laughed at Keira's disappointment.

You know every person in the group, our gifts, and our plans." Keira gasped.

"Erin, how could you choose the dark realm?"

"Samael recruited me long before Marion had chosen me for your mission. Acting as a bumbling idiot was quite convincing, don't you think?"

"Erin, your English pronunciation has disappeared."

"That's right. I did not think you would notice. After all, the word is you have never been the sharpest knife in the drawer."

"What childish behavior," said Marion.

"I will deal with you later, old lady."

Marion stepped forward to teach Erin a lesson in civility. But Osric quickly grabbed his mother's wrist and stopped her. "Later, mother," he whispered.

"I knew you were up to no good the day I saw you with Laurence in the cafeteria. Delivering Laurence to Abadon was one of your duties as well?"

"Yes, it was. Laurence was the perfect specimen. Celina will be even more treacherous and ruthless than her predecessors when she takes over my throne," said Erin.

Osric was concerned that Keira would struggle to drive the dagger through Erin's heart. Erin was banking on it. He gradually moved Keira aside, his blade hidden in his shirt sleeve, and introduced himself.

"Osric at your service."

His thoughts penetrated her mind with dark sexual imagery.

"I understand you can become my wildest fantasy," said Erin.

Erin realized that Osric could become a great asset.

Osric looked at her in a way that would make any woman melt.

"I always work very, very hard at pleasing my mate."

"Later, please show me more," said Erin.

Osric moved closer to the newly appointed mistress, his lips a breath away from her neck, and plunged the knife through her heart. The look of surprise in Erin's black empty eyes was something he would never forget.

"Yes, Erin, I never disappoint," said Osric.

Celina lifted her hood over her head and was ready to disappear. Hannah's knife spiraled through the air and took Celina's head off in one clean sweep.

Devon jumped Forrester and lost his grip on the knife.

Forrester had his knee on Devon's chest and began to strangle him.

"Idiot, you cannot kill me." Devon laughed.

"Why not?" Forrester grunted

"Because he is already dead," said Keira plunging the dagger into his heart.

"Maxime, immortality is off the table now that Erin is dead. You have two choices. You either give me the pleasure of cutting off your head or jail, said Keira."

Maxine angrily replied. "I guess jail is my only option. Keira, why did you refuse me that night? Where you suspicious?"

"Maxine, I am asexual. No one is my type."

With a wisp of her hand, Keira sent Maxine to a maximum detention center for life.

Hannah's facial features were back to normal, and she appeared to be her old self again.

"Hannah, you are beautiful again," Osric uttered.

"A broken heart can make a person go mad until the suitable salve is applied.

Keira, I am proud of you. I knew you would be strong."

Hannah removed a gold box from her pocket and handed it to Keira. "This is my Laurence's spirit. You know what to do," said Hannah.

Keira carefully placed the golden box in her pocket. "Hannah, when the war is over, Laurence and Devon will return."

"Keira, I need to be brought back before the war ends. I have some unfished business," said Devon.

Devon got up from his chair, ready to return to the upper realm.

"Dad, soon we will all be together again."

"Sadly, my time is up. We will see each other again one day, but, for now, I must go back."

"I love you so much, and I will always be here when you need me."

Then Devon vanished, leaving behind the clothing he wore.

"Mom, what now?"

Marion smiled. "It is time that we all go home. We have one more journey to complete. Abadon must die, and his kingdom destroyed."

"Keira, everyone has their bedtime snack. Are you coming?" Asked Hannah.

"Hannah, before we join the others, I have something for you. Bring your hands together as though you are ready to drink water from them."

Hannah followed Keira's instructions to the letter. A gold box appeared in Hannah's hands.

"Keira, what should I do with this?"

"Hannah, I know what has been going on between you and my dad. Every time you see each other, your feelings grow stronger. This box holds his life essence, and when you are ready, light a gold candle, face the flame, and repeat these words seven times. Essentia Lucis Renovamini."

"Keira, how did you find out about Essentia Lucis Renovamini? The essence of Light is Renewed."

"I have all of Headmaster's knowledge, and when it's time to use it, I instinctively remember. If anything happens to me, you can bring my father back," said Keira.

"Don't speak like that. Your safe with us," said Hannah.

"Hannah, go ahead and join the others. I will be in soon," said Keira.

Keira walked over to the fireplace and added wood to the ambers.

"Good idea; hardwood will burn through the night."

"Wanton, how did you get in?" asked Keira.

"The hatred you all shared seeing my servants die was like a personal invitation to come in while you were killing them off, said Wanton."

"I saw you leave the night Samael defeated you. I wondered when we would meet again. The show has ended, and I'm getting too old for your nonsense. I am going to end this fight tonight," Keira decreed.

In Keira's hand appeared an iron box.

I'm not the little girl you tried to possess a long time ago. Do you remember the night you wanted to rape me? It would have been the end of my life. You infected my body with your vile venom to weaken my will and get me pregnant. If you had succeeded, I would have lost my kingdom. Our kingdoms have been at odds for many years. Now is the time to end it. A golden mist surrounds Keira. She held out her hand, and the iron box opened.

"Wanton, it is time to join your son."

"You can't make me vanish as if I never existed."

Two golden serpents held Wanton in their coiled bodies and placed him in his prison. Headmaster appeared at her side.

"You have succeeded, my lovely Queen."

"We succeeded, Headmaster?"

"You defeated the darkness, Keira. As a proud grandfather, I stood back and watched."

"It takes courage to grow up and become who you are."
E.E. Cummings

The End

Printed in the United States
by Baker & Taylor Publisher Services